CRITTERS
FLITTERS & SPITTERS

CRITTERS
FLITTERS & SPITTERS

24

AMAZING
OHIO ANIMAL TALES

RICK SOWASH
Storyteller of the Heartland

Designed & Illustrated by Randall Wright

Rick Sowash Publishing Company
Cincinnati, Ohio

Rick Sowash Publishing Company
338 Milton Street
Cincinnati, Ohio 45202
Editorial and business office: (513) 721-1241
E-mail: rick@sowash.com

Manufactured in the United States of America.

To learn more about author Rick Sowash, go to www.sowash.com.

Publisher's Cataloguing-in-Publication Data
Sowash, Rick, 1950 -
    Critters, Flitters and Spitters: 24 Amazing Ohio Animal Tales / Rick Sowash;
illustrated by Randall Wright. 138 p. Includes index.
    0-9762412-3-4 Hardbound: $19.95.
    0-9762412-2-6 Softbound: $11.95.
Animals - Ohio.
2006.

Fourth Printing

Dedication

To my wife Jo, who has always loved animals,
and to the memory of Binsche, the best dog we ever had.

CONTENTS

Part I – Animals of Very Long Ago

1 Trilobite   1
2 Woolly Mammoth   7
3 Serpent Mound   13
4 Possum Fable   19

Part II – Animals of History

5 Little Turtle   25
6 General Sheridan's "Rienzi"   31
7 Passenger Pigeons   37
8 The Wright Family's Robin   43

Part III – Animals of Farm and Field

9 Cy Gatton and the Chicken That Ate Lightning Bugs   49
10 American Bald Eagles   55
11 Louis Bromfield's Remarkable Pig   61
12 Muskrat Attack—An Amish Story   67

Part IV – Animals Not Expected in Ohio

13 The Wilds   73
14 Hellbender   79
15 Zebra Mussels   85
16 Ohio's Elephants   91

Part V – People Helping Animals

17 Ohio Bird Sanctuary   97
18 Toad Tuning at Cedar Bog   103
19 Canada Geese   109
20 Guide Dogs   115

Part VI – Animals Helping People

21 Guide Horses   121
22 Search and Rescue Dogs   127
23 A Hero Named LuLu   133
24 Bud the Wonder Dog   139

Index   144

The Author   147

Acknowledgments / Picture Credits   148

Y ou just never know where ideas might come from, and it's amazing what can happen once they sprout. In the spring of 2001 I was in one of my favorite places, a school library, doing one of my favorite things, talking to kids. This particular school was in Cleveland Heights, and the kids were fifth-graders who were there to meet a real live author.

In these programs I talk a bit about my life and my work and about the two other books I've written: *Ripsnorting Whoppers* and *Heroes of Ohio*. Then comes the fun part when the kids get to ask questions. This is fun for me because I pretty much know what I'm going to say. After all, I've done lots and lots of these programs. But you never know what might come from the imagination of a youngster. On this particular day a girl named Emily asked why *Heroes of Ohio* didn't have any stories about ANIMAL heroes. "Animal heroes?"

"Well, it's a book about people," I said, "and what would make an animal a hero anyway? But wait! Yes, I can see it now! The gerbil that saved Cleveland Heights!" Of course everyone laughed, but right away I started thinking more about her question, and lots of interesting ideas came into my head.

I got busy and asked some friends to help with research. Over the next year, sure enough, a book took shape. Some of these stories are about real animals and real historical events, and some sprout from my imagination. Sometimes animals are the stars, and sometimes they only have a little part. But in this book, just like in life, animals are everywhere. And what an interesting bunch they are, with so much to teach us!

These Ohio animals are important in our geography, history and environment. They have influenced different cultures and ethnic groups in Ohio. Interesting animals are found on farms and in cities, in parks and special preserves. And animals really are heroic sometimes, not to mention scary and funny, sweet and sad. Just read these stories and see!

Like questions in the minds of kids, animals are always around, just waiting to get those wheels turning in our heads. So thanks, Emily, for your great question. And thanks to all the folks in schools and libraries and lots of other places who answer the questions we've got and give us so many more fun questions to think about.

A word about the title of this book. "Critters" is an old pioneer word for "creatures". "Flitters" are animals that flit, flutter and fly—birds, in other words. And by "Spitters," I mean animals that live by sucking in water, keeping the food particles, then spitting out the rest. The trilobite was a spitter as are zebra mussels.

There you have it: Critters, Flitters and Spitters!

Trilobite

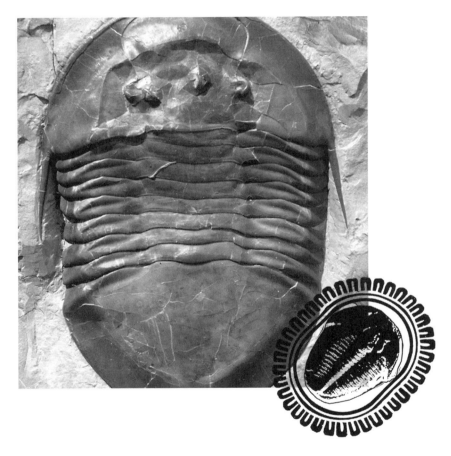

*There's a heap of fossils in this old world.
But not every fossil gets to be the official fossil
of a state. Here's how one little trilobite
made it to the big time.*

Something big, black and very scary was coming near and fast! Strong claws ripped through the muddy ocean floor. Desperate to escape, the little trilobite dove deep into the dark silt. Strong jaws snapped shut just above him. The little guy instantly pulled his legs to his belly and curled up in a tight ball. Then? Nothing. The hungry thing that had tried to eat him— whatever it was—had moved on. Such was life in Ohio 440 million years ago.

The trilobite slowly uncurled and went back to his own meal. Using his cheeks as shovels, he drew in a long slurp of yummy, salty mud. No, don't make a yucky face! It wasn't just dirt, that mud. There were good bits in it like tiny plants and animals. He spit out the dirt, but he kept the good stuff inside, the stuff that helped him grow.

And, slurping and spitting, grow he did. He had no backbone or inner skeleton. He had something better. He had an exoskeleton, a shell that was strong and flexible, like our fingernails. When his body got too big for his exoskeleton, he just squirmed out of it and grew a new, bigger exoskeleton. The longer he lived, the more shells he grew and shed and grew again.

So he lived. He ate, grew, dodged enemies and swam, his rows of legs pumping him forward. He had a happy life so long as he didn't get eaten.

Our hero had millions of relatives. In those days there were more trilobites on earth than you could believe. The trilobites' distant cousins are still around today—crabs, lobsters and shrimp, to name a few.

Then, about 250 million years ago, trilobites died out. No one knows why. But don't think of them as an experiment that failed.

They were here for 310 million years. Humans have been around for one million years. That means we've got to last another 309 million years before we catch up with the trilobites. (Do you think we'll make it?)

Back to our hero. He was lucky! Somehow he never got eaten. He grew and grew until he got to be one of the biggest trilobites. He was almost as big as a toilet seat when he finally died of old age. His body settled into the muddy sea floor that had been his home and was buried in silt. There it lay for 440 million years as the mud and silt turned to stone.

Then one hot July day in 1919... "Holy Moses, Charlie! Take a look at *this*!" Charlie looked where Frank was pointing. Then he dropped his shovel. His eyes grew wide. He puffed out his cheeks. "It's the biggest dang bug I ever seen!" he said. "That ain't no bug, you chump, it's a fossil! Quick! Get the boss over here."

Their boss came. He was Mr. Arthur Morgan. He planned and built the dams that were to save Dayton from floods. His young son loved fossils and he told the workers to look for them as they dug. He was very surprised by this fossil. He wiped the sweat off his bald head, pushed his glasses higher on his nose and bent nearer. "It's a whole trilobite—and the largest one I ever heard of!" he whooped.

The trilobite fossil became famous. You can see it today in the Smithsonian Institution in Washington, D.C. But the story doesn't end on a museum shelf. Let's pick up the tale again in 1985.

Third-grader Gary Midkiff looked at his reflection in the glass display case at the Dayton Museum of Natural History. A stiff sweep of his blond hair stuck straight up. That darned cowlick! Then he looked through the glass at the copy of the famous trilobite. His third grade teacher had bragged about it. Ms. Doris Swabb had told them how big it was and how it was found and saved by the workers who built Huffman Dam. That's why it was called the Huffman Dam Trilobite. Gary stared and stared. The thing was weird, all right. It was huge, creepy and definitely impressive.

Gary's classmates in the Beavertown School third grade were also excited about the Huffman Dam Trilobite—and not just because it was so old and so big. These kids in Kettering were on a quest along with Ms. Virginia Evers' fourth graders at St. Anthony's School in Dayton. The two classes wanted to make the trilobite even more famous. They wanted to make it the official state fossil of Ohio. Ohio had a state bird, a state flower, even a state drink (it's tomato juice). Time for a state fossil!

Ms. Swabb had heard that New York was choosing a state fossil. "Ohio should do the same," she thought, "because the biggest trilobite *ever* was found right here!"

The kids wrote letters to the state legislature. They got help from many clubs, museums and nature centers. News of their campaign spread. Even people in far off countries offered to help. A lot of people love trilobite fossils. Many come very far to search for them in southwestern Ohio.

The kids went to the legislature in Columbus and made speeches. Ms. Evers' class passed out trilobite-shaped peanut-butter cookies to the 99 legislators. The teachers asked the legislators to remember how it was when they were third graders. Ms. Swabb added, "Most Ohioans have once had, when they were kids, a shoebox full of fossils which they would not let their mothers throw out!"

The legislators ate the cookies and scratched their heads. A trilobite? A state fossil? Why not?

Gary Midkiff and 200 other school kids and parents from Ms. Swabb's and Ms. Evers' schools were right there when Governor Dick Celeste signed the bill into law. (The bill said that *all* members of the trilobite's genus group could be official state fossils.) Gary's cowlick still stuck up, but he didn't care. He was too proud—proud of the kids, proud of the teachers, but mostly proud of the trilobite.

To learn more…
Dwight and the Trilobite by Kelli C. Foster, Kerri Gifford and Gina Clegg Erickson (Get Ready-Get Set-Read!, 1994)

For adult readers: *Trilobite: Eyewitness to Evolution* by Richard A. Fortey (Alfred A. Knopf, 2000)

Web sites
http://community-1.webtv.net/mrbbug/MrBBugsTrilobite (a trilobite web site for kids, complete with Jurassic Park theme music)

www.ohiodnr.com/geosurvey/geo_fact/geo_f06.htm (includes a photograph of the fossil)

www.gardengrow.com/info/Science/Earth_Sciences/Paleontology/Invertebrates/Arthropods/Trilobites/~13k (provides useful links)

http://newdeal.feri.org/bios/bio2.htm (more about Arthur E. Morgan, who went on to be the first director of the Tennessee Valley Authority)

www.dayton.net/Audubon/hufman.htm (Dayton's Huffman Metropark)

www.boonshoftmuseum.org (Dayton's Museum of Discovery)

www.oplin.lib.oh.us/products/ohiodefined/ohd-13.html (tomato juice, the official state drink)

2

Woolly Mammoth

*Nobody messes with a woolly mammoth.
Not anymore. Hey, they're extinct! But even
when they were around, it wasn't too smart
to get too close to a woolly mammoth...*

He was minding his own business. He knew he was big, but he wasn't in anybody's way. He didn't ask much, just some scattered patches of grass to eat, melted snow to drink. Once in a while his thoughts turned toward the females. Basically though, he just wanted to be left alone.

Yet here they came again, pestering him. Most animals left him alone. And he left them alone. But not these. They were different. Pale, nasty, stinky little creatures. He could smell them a mile away. Phew! Long tangles of black hair grew from out of the tops of their tiny heads. They wrapped their scrawny selves in dead skins, just to keep warm. They were dangerous, too. He could sense that. In their hairless, grasping little claws, they carried long sticks with sharply pointed stones tied to one end.

They were still a long way off, fanning out but drawing slowly nearer. He could hear their squeaky voices, planning and plotting. He began to move away from them.

Among the puddles in the snowy plain up ahead, he spotted clumps of long, green grass left over from the short summer. Ah, sweet grass! He loved the stuff. Good thing because he had to eat at least 300 pounds of grass every day. (That's like eight big garbage pails filled with lawn clippings!) That was how he built up the thick layer of fat he needed to get through the long winters. And winter was just now beginning. Soon he'd be using his long tusks to plow down under the snow for buried scraps of dried grasses. But he wasn't worried. A shaggy coat of long, dark red hair grew out of his tough, furry, inch-thick skin. That helped keep him warm. But fat was what he really needed. And he got fat by eating grass and leaves whenever he could find them.

There were other woolly mammoths around, whole herds of

them, with mothers and babies. He stayed away from them. He liked to be alone. So did all the other male mammoths. It was their way.

His heavy feet crunched the snow underfoot as he walked toward the grass. His front legs were much longer than his back legs. He was built for marching and could go 50 miles in a single day. When he felt tired, he could lie down to sleep, slowly folding his legs and slumping to the ground. Or he could nap standing up. The tracks he left in the snow showed four short nails on each foot. The coldness of the snow didn't bother his feet. With thick, fleshy pads on the bottoms of his feet, he couldn't even feel the cold.

As far as he was concerned, let the cold come! Let the Ice Age come! Bring on the glaciers, those great walls of ice, a mile thick, sliding out of the far, frozen north, scooping out Lake Erie like a giant bulldozer and pushing all the dirt south. He was ready.

It was snowing when he reached the clumps of grass. He yanked up a sheaf with his trunk and curled it back in his mouth. The snow melted pleasantly on his warm, rough, pink tongue. He ground the sweet, green stuff between teeth as big and strong as bricks. Ah, yum!

But here they were again, those disgusting creatures. He raised his great, dome-shaped head. He could move his head up and down, but he had to turn to look sideways. He turned now and saw them running toward him, waggling their spears.

So that was their game…they meant to do him harm! It wasn't the first time. Once they tried to run him off a cliff. Another time they tried to drive him into deep mud where he might get stuck, and then they could spear him. He knew their tricks. He was almost 70 years old, more than twice as old as the oldest of these puny creatures. He was smarter than they thought. And he was twice as tall and weighed nine tons, heavier than one hundred men!

For that is what the creatures were, of course: men. Hungry, scared, needy men. They didn't hunt him for fun but because they were desperate. They needed his body to keep their families alive. They needed his meat to eat and preserve for the long winter. They needed his skin and tusks. They needed his large bones to use as tent poles for their shelters. They even needed his small bones to splinter into needles to sew skins together for clothes and to carve into fish hooks. No other animal was so useful, so slow, so easy to find on the open, icy, grassy plains. There was just one problem. No other animal was as dangerous to hunt.

He looked around him. No cliffs were near and no deep mud. He ignored the men and yanked up more grass. Suddenly he felt a small stab of pain in his right side. He jerked sideways. One man was very near and there was red blood on the sharp stone tip of his stick. *His* blood! All the other men were running fast, closing in.

A hot rage shivered through him from trunk to tail. He turned right, facing the man who had stabbed him. The man was backing away, still threatening with his bloody spear. What to do? He charged. The man stumbled back and fell to a sitting position. Before the man could rise, the mammoth deftly swung his massive 13-foot tusks upward. (Each tusk was as big as half a telephone pole.) He hooked the man in the ribs and tossed him, screaming, high into the air. To the mammoth the man weighed almost nothing.

Two other men suddenly closed in from the left, stabbing at

his thick hide. He swung at them with his tusks. Both ducked, but one slipped and fell on his back. The mammoth raised his front leg and brought it crashing down on the man's chest. To the mammoth the man seemed as soft and squishy as a puddle of mud. The other man rolled over and over in the snow, trying to escape. The mammoth bellowed and again raised his massive leg but suddenly felt spear-stings near his tail. He was getting really angry now.

He whirled about more quickly this time, stretching his neck. His tusks mowed down men like cattails. Then he reared up on his hind legs and let loose a wild, trumpeting blast. It echoed across the freezing plain.

The remaining men turned and ran hard. Their families would be hungry tonight, but they could do no more in the darkening of this blustery day.

The mammoth watched them fade into the thickness of the falling snow. Then he turned back to the grassy clump to prepare for the winter ahead.

To learn more...

Wild and Woolly Mammoths by Aliki (HarperCollins Juvenile Books, 1998)
A Woolly Mammoth Journey by Debbie S. Miller (Little Brown & Company, 2001)
The Mystery of the Mammoth Bones and How It Was Solved by James Cross Giblin (HarperCollins Children's Books, 1999)
Native Americans by Laura Buller (Secret Worlds, A Dorling Kindersley Book, 2001)
For adult readers: *Mammoth* by Adrian Lister and Paul Bahn (Macmillan, 1994)

Web sites
www.zoomdinosaurs.com/subjects/mammals/mammoth (includes printouts)
http://dsc.discovery.com/convergence/landofmammoth/landofmammoth.html
    (an interactive Ice Age journey)
www.mammothsite.com (provides useful links)
http://school.discovery.com/schooladventures/woollymammoth/weblinks.html (links)
www.amnh.org/exhibitions/expeditions/siberia/ (American Museum of Natural
    History's 1998 expedition to help understand why mammoths died out)

3

Serpent Mound

Nobody knows why Native Americans
labored to build a monster snake
on some gentle hills in Adams County.
But sometimes it's fun to try to solve
an ancient and magnificent mystery.

A young man was digging into the forest floor. The damp, cool smell of the earth rose to his face. He wasn't digging with a metal shovel, for The People had no such tools. He was digging with a clamshell and pushing the dirt into a deer-skin sack.

When the sack was full, he hoisted it onto his shoulder and stood. His skin was as reddish-brown as a copper penny, and it glistened in the sun. He was covered with sweat. It trickled out from his long black hair and down his forehead. Droplets gathered on his nose and slid down onto his lips. He licked his lips. He liked the salty taste of his sweat.

He wore only a loincloth and moccasins—no shirt, no shoes, no pants. The People were Native Americans and lived a little ways north of the Ohio River about 1,000 years ago.

He carried his sack of dirt along a path. Beauty was all around him. Sunbeams poured through the leaves overhead and fell in trembling yellow spots on mossy rocks and lush ferns.

Other workers fell into place ahead and behind him on the path. Another line moved alongside them, going the opposite direction with empty sacks.

As they walked, both lines joined in a solemn song in a language no one knows today. Their proud voices echoed through a tiny corner of the vast, ancient forest that covered the land. The People sang of the great spirits they worshipped and especially of the Snake Spirit. It was for the Snake Spirit that they gathered these thousands of sacks of dirt.

At the end of the path rose a mound of fresh dirt. The young man emptied his sack onto the mound and turned to go back and fill it again. The People were building this mound. But it was not to be a simple, round mound. It was to be in the shape of a giant snake, a quarter of a mile long.

In time, the mound was finished. Its delicate curves were lovely to see. It showed a snake opening its jaws around an oval shape.

Why build a mound in the shape of a snake? I think The People knew exactly why. What purpose did it serve? The People all knew. I think they believed that it was the greatest, most important thing they had ever done. But they are gone now and no one can ask them to explain their serpent-shaped mound. Nobody will ever know the whole story.

The People cherished their serpent mound for a long, long time. Then times changed, and slowly the purpose of the mound was forgotten. When pioneers arrived 800 years later, they asked the local Native Americans about the mound. They could tell the newcomers nothing for sure. Through the years many people have put forth ideas about the snake-shaped mound. Some are silly explanations and some are clever, but of course none can "prove" why The People built it.

Then, a few years ago, some archaeologists suggested another theory. They based their theory on pieces from the mound that indicated that The People built it sometime between 1000 and 1100. Suddenly the Great Serpent Mound, as modern Ohioans call it, made sense. The date of its construction was the crucial clue. Why? Back to my story of The People and the Serpent— truly an amazing Ohio animal!

The People loved to watch the stars. There were no electric lights in the whole world back then and no haze of pollution to dim the stars. The stars shone brightly every night. Only clouds could hide them. The People knew every star, and they knew the exact path each star took as it wheeled slowly around the ever-fixed North Star. They knew how the sky shifted with the passing seasons. And they knew just where the sun would appear on the shortest day of the year, and on the longest day, and also on the day exactly half-way between those two days. All this they knew with absolute certainty. The night sky was as predictable as the sun rising in the East.

Then one night the sky did change. They saw something that no one remembered ever seeing before. Was it a new star? They eagerly waited for the next night. It was there again, a little brighter. Each night it grew bigger and brighter. The People were terribly confused and excited. Was it a good omen or a sign of coming evil? What could it mean?

Then the new star began to grow a tail. And it outshone all of the other stars. Each night The People looked in wonder and terror at the sky, hoping the new star would shrink. But it grew steadily bigger and brighter. Even the oldest of The People could remember nothing like it. (It wasn't only The People who noticed it. Europeans saw it too. They recorded it in history in 1066, around the time Serpent Mound was being built. Today we call it Halley's Comet.)

Finally, The People decided what it was. To them it was the Snake Spirit. It was hungry and it was traveling toward them. It would eat The People along with the forest, the river and everything. What could be done to stop it?

The wisest of The People thought deeply. "Build a giant snake here on the earth," they advised. "And when the Snake Spirit looks down and sees this giant snake, he will see that The People honor him. He will see that The People honor the stars and the sun and the times of their coming and going. And he will have mercy and will not devour The People, the forest, or the river."

Thus, The People labored and built the Serpent Mound to honor the power of the sun and stars. Its curves show just where the sun will rise on the shortest day, on the longest day, and also on the day half-way between those two days. And the plan seemed to work. As the mound took on its serpent shape, the Snake Spirit began to fade. Its tail grew shorter, its head grew dimmer. Finally, it disappeared altogether.

The People had done it. Their Serpent Mound had helped turn the path of the Snake Spirit and saved the world, or so they thought. And why not? What do you think?

To learn more...
Indian Mounds of the Middle Ohio Valley by Susan Woodward and Jerry McDonald (McDonald and Woodward Publishing, 2002)
Halley's Comet: What We've Learned by Gregory Vogt (F. Watts, 1987)
For adult readers: *Serpent Mound: Ohio's Enigmatic Effigy Mound* by Robert C. Glotzhober and Bradley T. Lepper (Ohio Historical Society, 1994) includes the astronomical alignments mentioned in this story

Web sites
www.ohiohistory.org/places/serpent (visit, or call 937-587-2796 or 800-752-2757)
www.ohiokids.org/asafari.html (select Serpent Mound)
www.sunwatch.org (SunWatch archaeological site, 1200 AD, also purports to include astronomical alignments)
www.500nations.com/Ohio_Places.asp (Native American sites to visit in Ohio)

www.getty.edu/artsednet/resources/Space/Stories/halleys.html (shows the Bayeux
   Tapestry and Halley's Comet as seen in Europe in 1066)
www.windows.ucar.edu/tour/link=/comets/Halleys_comet.html (offers more information about Halley's Comet and its return visit to the earth in 2061)

4

Possum Fable

*A fable is a short tale, usually with animals
as characters, that teaches a moral. This fable offers us
the wisdom, humor and rhythm of Native American
storytelling. So get off your chair and onto your feet
and prepare to follow along.*

Fred Shaw, of Milford, Ohio, is a Shawnee storyteller. Back when times were tough for American Indians in Ohio, Fred's ancestors took "Shaw" as their last name to disguise the word "Shawnee." As Fred says, "They just dropped the 'nee' and said goodbye to the soldiers." These days Fred likes to be known as Fred Shaw/Neeake. Neeake is Shawnee for Canada goose and can mean "He-Talks-as-He-Flies," a good name for a storyteller, especially a Shawnee storyteller. As Fred explains, "The way stories are told among my people is that the teller simply permits the story to move through him or her. As I tell a story, I move the way the story directs. Storytelling is very close to dance in my culture."

Many Eastern Woodlands people share a traditional story about the opossum, or possum. Here is how Fred Shaw/Neeake tells it—and how he moves when he tells it. I've arranged it so you can act it out or have a friend help you.

The Grandfathers and the Grandmothers tell us that, long ago[1], the possum was a very beautiful creature. He had lovely, long white fur[2]. Whenever his fur caught the light, there were sparkles and rainbows in it[3]. But most beautiful of all was his long tail. Possum had a way of draping it so that it would always catch the light[4]. Whenever he walked, his tail would swish, swish, swish[5]!

He was beautiful, and he knew it[6]. He made sure others knew it, too[7]. He would say, "Do you see my tail? Is it not a beautiful tail?

[1] glance backward over your right shoulder, into the past time
[2] stroke down your side with your right hand
[3] fingers of your right hand dance outward and then your hand moves in a rainbow arc
[4] extend your right arm backward with a gesture as if draping a silk cloth over your tail
[5] wiggle your hips while walking and wag your hand and arm behind like a graceful tail
[6] tilt your head to one side and caress down the lower side
[7] tell it as you look directly at your audience

See how the light is in it[8]?" All the people would say, "Yes, yes, Possum, we see your tail, Possum. And yes, yes, it's a beautiful tail, Possum[9]!!"

Finally his friends got to talking[10]. "Possum is a fine fellow," they said, "but he thinks too much of himself. We are his friends, and we should help him[11]." Rabbit and Squirrel made a plan[12]. They came to him and said, "Everyone knows of your beautiful tail[13]. There should be a dance held in its honor. We have brought with us Cricket[14]. He will comb your tail[15] until it shines and glows in the dark[16]. He will wrap it with a soft buckskin ribbon to keep it clean until the time of the dance[17]. You must not touch it[18]. We don't want even the slightest crease in that beautiful tail.[19]"

Cricket went to work. Possum puffed up all the more[20]. He forgot that Cricket is also called The Barber because he likes to sneak in at night and take a little of your hair to remember you[21]. So as he combed, Cricket snipped every hair at the

---

[8] *lift your hand and hold out your tail for all to admire*

[9] *bow slightly and begin nodding your head way up and way down as you gradually grit your teeth*

[10] *open your arms to your listeners, to invite them into your plan*

[11] *move right hand, palm up, from your heart out to include everyone who'll help, and then back to yourself*

[12] *clasp your hands at chest level*

[13] *raise your open hands toward Possum*

[14] *extend your right hand out and downward, to present Cricket (remember, he's small)*

[15] *make a soft combing gesture*

[16] *look upward in joy with your hands opening up and away from your face*

[17] *make a wrapping motion*

[18] *hold your right palm up and out, as if you are stopping traffic*

[19] *reach back and smooth out and caress your tail*

[20] *swell your chest and swagger a little*

[21] *pretend to hold up a lock of hair, cut it with your sharp knife, then tuck the lock inside your shirt pocket*

root[22] and caught each one in the soft buckskin ribbon so that it would not fall on the ground[23]. When he was all done, he said, "Now remember, Possum, do not touch the ribbon until the time of the dance[24]."

Then a great fire was lit[25], and Possum came out to dance. He began to strut around the outside of the circle[26]. "Soon you will see it, soon you will see my beautiful tail," he gloated.

Then he danced into the center of the circle[27]. "Now you will see it, now you will see my tail!"

He danced ever harder, swishing his tail[28]. Then he reached behind him and pulled the ribbon off[29]. A great shout went up, and he knew that they were impressed[30]. He danced all the harder. "Now you see it, is it not a wonderful tail?" he kept saying.

Then a young animal child pointed and said in a high, shrill voice[31], "Look at his tail! Look at his tail! There's no hair[32]!"

Possum looked behind[33], and all he saw was an ugly[34] pink[35]

[22] *hold the hair with your left hand and make small cutting motions with your right hand*
[23] *make a wrapping motion*
[24] *pat Possum on his back*
[25] *pretend the fire is in the center of your listeners and, watching the center, bring your hands up from your waist, palms up, flowing up and outward like leaping flames*
[26] *strut about with your right hand pointing backward to your tail—but do not turn your head toward it*
[27] *move with a swooping dance, still keeping your right arm and hand back as if supporting your tail*
[28] *just strut and swish that tail!*
[29] *suddenly pull, ripping the ribbon from your tail*
[30] *puff up even more, smile, and keep looking forward*
[31] *speak this in a high child-like voice*
[32] *make your eyes big, form your mouth in a big O-shape, and point in astonishment*
[33] *let the horror slowly spread across your face and body*
[34] *point!*
[35] *point!*

stick[36] rising out of his rump[37]. He was so surprised and so embarrassed that he fell down in a faint—right into the fire[38]!

His friends pulled him out[39] but not before his long and beautiful coat had been singed ragged and short by the fire[40] and had changed to the color of the ashes and the smoke[41].

He lay there squinting his eyes shut in his great embarrassment[42]. He wished he were dead, and he grinned a death's smile[43]. But then his friends said, "It's all right, Possum. We are still with you. You do not have to be dead[44]."

From that day to this, Possum's hair never has grown back on his tail[45]. His fur looks like he has just been pulled from the fire[46]. And if you surprise him, he will seem to faint...and just lie there grinning, pretending he's dead[47].

But now, thanks to his friends, Possum truly *IS* a very fine fellow[48].

[36] point!

[37] bring your pointing index finger up from the tail position, turn your head and focus on your finger until it is close to your face and you are cross-eyed!

[38] bend up your right arm at the elbow and then let it fall over toward the central area where you "built" the fire

[39] make a dragging-from-the-fire motion

[40] make short, backhand strokes down your sides as if stroking something nasty

[41] curl your upper lip and flare your nostrils as if you are smelling something awful

[42] squint and hide your head in your shoulders

[43] make a big, hideous toothy grin

[44] hug your shoulders in encouragement

[45] shake your head slowly and sadly

[46] make a pulling-from-the-fire motion

[47] hunch up your shoulders and grin with one eye peeking out to see if anyone is there

[48] stand straight and tall with a big smile

To learn more...

Why the Possum's Tail Is Bare and Other North American Indian Nature Tales compiled and edited by James E. Connolly (Stemmer House Publishers, 1994)

The Opossum by Emily Crofford (Crestwood House, 1990)

Web sites

www.monvalleyhistory.com/fas/ (Fred Shaw/Neeake enjoys making school visits, or contact him by telephone 513-576-6002 or email at fashaw@juno.com)

http://www.kidsbooksandpuppets.com/Folkmanis/opossumbp.html (possum books and puppets)

5

Little Turtle

Sometimes, depending on how much you know, little events can start your mind remembering all sorts of things. Here's a tale of an ordinary reptile that reminded me of the history of Little Turtle—an amazing story of a great man with an animal name.

Something was moving on the pavement ahead. It was a turtle, trundling his way across the highway, never dreaming of danger. I glanced in my rear-view mirror to check that nobody was behind me. The shoulder of the road was wide just there, next to the woods. So I pulled over and got out.

He (or was it a she?) was a charming creature, about as big around as a grapefruit. He had a fancy olive-green shell with delicate lines and flecks of yellow and orange. His head was straining forward while his feet clawed the asphalt. I moved in behind him and gingerly picked him up between my thumb and middle finger. Surprised, he stretched his neck and made frantic crawling motions. I was careful to keep my other fingers clear of his straining beak and scrabbling claws. I set him down in the woods, facing him away from the highway.

As I watched him go, I said, "Goodbye, little turtle." Then it struck me. Capitalize the "l" and "t" and you get "Little Turtle," the Indian commander from the Miami nation who taught the American army a terrible lesson at the battle known as St. Clair's Defeat. On that day unexpected things happened, and it was the Native Americans who surprised—and defeated—U.S. troops. And it was right in Mercer County, Ohio, not far from where I stood by the highway.

American settlers and soldiers thought Native Americans would only attack in small war parties, making raids on lonely cabins. They never dreamed the various tribes could gather a whole regiment of warriors, let alone attack a U.S. Army camp. So, in 1791 Congress and President George Washington confidently ordered gray-haired Arthur St. Clair, Governor of the Northwest Territory and a general of the U.S. Army, to lead his troops into the woods north of Cincinnati. His assignment was to end the "Indian problem" once and for all.

General St. Clair was ill and often had to be carried on a litter. His army was smaller than he wanted and full of fresh recruits. Their supplies were unreliable. Their guns were old, their food was moldy and a cheating crook had sold them boxes of sand marked "gunpowder." The grumbling soldiers were dressed for summer, but they didn't march until autumn was chilling the air. There was no road north. They slashed their way through the woods, cutting a wide trail. Twice they stopped for two weeks to build forts. Men were quitting every day, sneaking out of camp to return home.

But the struggling army did not know that all through late summer and fall Indian warriors had gathered. They were 1,400 strong, members of the Miami, Wyandot, Ottawa, Shawnee, Delaware, Chippewa, Potawatomi. All had sent warriors. Some were famous or would become so. Black Hoof (Shawnee) and Tarhe the Crane (Wyandot) were there as well as two white men who hated the American settlers, Blue Jacket (Shawnee) and Simon Girty (Seneca). Among Little Turtle's scouts was a 21-year-old Shawnee named Tecumseh. His older brother had made a famous claim: "The white man is a monster who is always hungry and what he eats is land!"

Little Turtle divided his force into 70 groups of 20 warriors each. They made a loose circle around St. Clair's shrinking army. Then they followed, watched and waited. The scouts reported what they saw to Little Turtle. The wise Miami chief made plans. "Mishikinakwa" his people called him: "Wise, with a soul of fire."

The reports showed Little Turtle that General St. Clair made mistakes. First, he sent his best scouts out of camp—away from where they were most needed—to try to capture Indians for questioning. Second, when 60 soldiers sneaked off to go back to their homes in Kentucky, St. Clair sent 300 of his bravest men after them, down that isolated trail.

Finally, late in the afternoon of November 3, the weary American army made camp. (Today the Ohio town of Ft. Recovery sits on the very spot.) Up until that day, St. Clair had ordered his men to dig ditches and put up earthworks for protection every time they stopped for the night. But it was late and the men were tired and cold, so they made no defenses—and that was the most important mistake.

When Little Turtle learned of St. Clair's mistakes, he knew the time had come to be bold. St. Clair had only about 1,400 men left, so both sides were equal. Little Turtle ordered his 70 units to tighten their circle round the army camp during the night. There were to be no Indian campfires. "The fire of our hate for the white invader will be enough to keep us warm tonight," he said.

The attack came at dawn. Indians swept in from three sides. Right away they killed the gunners who manned the cannons. Little Turtle had ordered this because he knew that his warriors feared the large guns the most. Only two cannon shots were fired.

St. Clair was too sick to stand. He saddled up, but four horses were shot from under him. He crawled frantically, shouting orders. Little Turtle also gave orders. "Kill their leaders first," he said. Soon General Richard Butler, second in command, was dead along with most of the other officers. Eight bullets ripped through St. Clair's coat, but none found their mark and his life was spared.

Again and again, the Americans tried to break out of Little

Turtle's circle. The attackers would fall back but then hold firm. After two and a half hours Colonel William Darke's men, bayonets and swords flashing, finally punched an escape hole back to the newly-cut wilderness road. St. Clair and whoever else could run, walk or crawl followed. The retreat became a flight. Men dropped their rifles and ran blindly.

The Native Americans could have chased them and killed them all, easily picking them off one by one from the safety of the dense forest. But Little Turtle said no. It was enough that 913 U.S. soldiers were dead as well as many of the women and children who had tagged along. Incredibly, the Native Americans had lost only about 60 warriors. It was a major victory, but Little Turtle wondered if the Americans would learn anything from their defeat. Would the Americans remember to honor their agreements and keep out of the Indian lands?

St. Clair's Defeat was the worst defeat the U.S. Army had ever suffered. More soldiers were killed that day than in any of General George Washington's Revolutionary War battles. Strangely, the battle is hardly remembered. The Last Stand of Colonel George Custer (did you know he was from Ohio?), fought 85 years later, is much more famous. Yet Custer lost not even a third as many men as St. Clair.

Sometimes people forget history. Writers must remind them. But writers need reminders, too. Thinking of that, I looked for the little turtle I had surprised.

He had already fled. I wondered if he would remember me.

To learn more...

Little Turtle by Maggi Cunningham (Dillon Press, 1978)

For adult readers: *Kekionga!: The Worst Defeat in the History of the U.S. Army* by Wilbur Edel (Praeger, 1997)

Turtles by Martha E.H. Rustad (Pepple Books, 2002) turtles as pets

Tortoises by Jerry G. Wells (Chelsea House, 1998) natural history and care of turtles

Web sites

www.ohiokids.org/ohc/history/h_indian/people/lturtle.html (Little Turtle and the Shawnee)

www.shelbycountyhistory.org/schs/indians/chflittleturtle.htm (Little Turtle)

www.angelfire.com/realm/shades/nativeamericans/littleturtle.htm (Little Turtle and links)

www.scripps.ohiou.edu/seo/winter96/bluejckt.htm (Blue Jacket)

www.wyandot.org/tarhe.htm (Tarhe the Crane)

http://www.turtle-tracks.org/issue81/i81_13.html (Black Hoof)

http://earlyamerica.com/review/summer/battle.html (Arthur St. Clair)

www.ohiohistory.org/places/ftrecovr/ (arrange a visit to Ft. Recovery, or call 419-375-4649 or 800-283-8920)

6

General Sheridan's "Rienzi"

*The most famous Civil War horse was Robert E. Lee's
Traveler. Second comes Phil Sheridan's Rienzi,
made famous by the poem "Sheridan's Ride,"
written by Buchanan Read just a few blocks
from my home in Cincinnati...*

Rienzi heard it first, just before dawn. A distant rumble, like thunder, faintly shook the stable. The horse twitched his ears and shook the beautiful long black hair from his intelligent eyes. He was a war horse and he knew that sound. Cannons! He swished his tail. There would be action this day!

Sure enough, here came the orderly with blanket and saddle. The orderly was a little afraid of Rienzi. Most soldiers were a little afraid of him. They said he was too spirited. He certainly had too much energy for his first owner, a city-bred captain. The captain had given Rienzi to Phil Sheridan, a country man from Somerset, Ohio, and commander of the cavalry of the Union Army during the Civil War.

Sheridan came now, a little man, just under five and a half feet tall, with hair, mustache and goatee as black as his horse. In his kneeboots and brass-buttoned blue uniform he looked every inch the soldier. He was wearing his famous round short-brimmed hat.

Soon Sheridan and his officers were riding past the red brick buildings and white clapboard houses of Winchester, Virginia. At the edge of town, they heard the sound again, closer this time. Cannons were firing near Cedar Creek, twelve miles away. What did it mean?

Sheridan bent over the pommel of his saddle to listen. The roaring was faint, but it didn't stop. The horsemen moved ahead a half mile at a steady gait. Then Sheridan dismounted, kneeled, and put his ear to the ground to listen, Indian-style. The cannon thunder was getting closer.

Rienzi knew something was up. He could tell by the way his rider remounted and spurred him. Rienzi's big hooves clip-clopped across the bridge over Mill Creek, then pounded the dust as the column rode uphill.

Topping the crest, they saw a staggering sight. A whole army of panic-stricken Union soldiers were rushing toward them like a mighty blue wave. Hundreds were wounded and hundreds more were unhurt but fear-struck. Many had dropped their weapons in terror and confusion. Supply wagons choked the road, forcing men and horses out into the fields on either side. All were fleeing headlong back to Winchester in hopeless confusion.

Rienzi heard an officer breathlessly reporting to Sheridan. "Surprise attack at dawn! Thousands of Confederate rebels coming at us! Headquarters captured! Everything gone! The army broken up, in full retreat!"

Sheridan was tense but calm and in control. Rienzi sensed this. It was why he loved his owner. They shared a special energy most didn't have. Rienzi longed to plunge ahead, to join the battle. But when Sheridan dismounted and walked, holding his reins, Rienzi followed patiently.

Sheridan was thinking what to do. Should he go back and make a last-ditch stand at Winchester? That's not how battles are won and Sheridan had never lost a battle. No, his place was up front with his men. He would plunge ahead and join the battle. He would do what he could in person to put back together his shattered army.

He set off with just two aides and 20 troopers. One trooper carried the general's famous double-pointed pennant: red star on white, white star on red. It snapped in the breeze as they made their way full speed ahead—to glory or disaster.

Sheridan set a swift yet sensible pace. It was still 10 miles to Cedar Creek but a good day for riding. Rusty-red autumn colors rolled down the mountain slopes, and the October skies were deepest blue. Sheridan easily kept 50 yards ahead of the rest, Rienzi's legs rippling with power.

At first they took to the fields to avoid the traffic jam of wagons and men on the road. Then after a couple of miles they got past the tangle and began to gallop down the road. Their dark blue uniforms soon powdered over with dust. In the excitement Rienzi's breath was hot and eager.

When soldiers resting at road's edge saw their commander heading for battle on his mighty black horse, they jumped up, threw their hats in the air and cheered. Then they picked up their muskets and followed. The news spread—Sheridan had come!

He could have shamed the men for retreating, but he just kept riding ahead, shouting, "Come on back, boys! Face the other way! We're going to lick those fellows out of their boots!"

Farther down the road, Newtown, Virginia, was so full of fugitives that Sheridan detoured around the village. That was where Major William McKinley, a future president—and from Ohio— spotted the general's pennant as his little column tore past. McKinley, too, spread the news.

Another future president—also from Ohio—Colonel Rutherford B. Hayes was among the soldiers still fighting the Confederates from behind a fence atop a small hill. He never forgot Sheridan's arrival. The little general jumped his horse over the fence and wheeled to face what was left of his army.

"Men, by God, we'll whip them yet!" Sheridan yelled as he rode along the crest, waving his little round hat. The men cheered back and raised their flags.

The famous ride was over. Sheridan dismounted, pointing at

the Confederate lines and barking orders. Rienzi had done his part. As the great horse was led away for a well-earned rub down, everyone knew what would happen next. Sheridan would strike back hard and turn defeat into victory.

To learn more...

Sheridan's Ride by Thomas Buchanan Read, illustrated by Nancy Winslow Parker (Greenwillow Books, 1993) also provides maps, background materials and battle flags of the Civil War

For adult readers: *Sheridan in the Shenandoah* by Edward J. Stackpole (Stackpole Books, 1992)

Web sites

www.si.edu/resource/faq/nmah/horse.htm (Rienzi is stuffed and on display in the Smithsonian Institution)

www.roadsideamerica.com/pet/steed.html (other famous horses in history)

www.eng.uci.edu/students/mpontius/hartley/187-187_.html (Read's poem and map)

www.thewildgeese.com/pages/sheridan.html (Phil Sheridan)

www.smithsonianmag.si.edu/smithsonian/issues96/nov96/object_nov96.html (background to Read's poem)

www.pe.net/~rksnow/ohcountysomerset.htm (information about Sheridan's statue)

7

Passenger Pigeons

When I told my nephew I was writing a book about amazing animals of Ohio, he asked me right away, "So, which is the most amazing?" I answered, "Well, it's hard to say, but the most amazing bird was certainly the passenger pigeon."

S ometimes a young person like you hears a story that changes everything and shapes your future. A relative, teacher or friend finds just the right words at just the right time. These words give you a great gift: a destiny to fulfill.

Long ago, around the end of the nineteenth century, Arlie Schorger's uncle found the right words at the right time. What a tale he told!

One day Arlie and his uncle were riding in a wagon to Kilbourne, Ohio. Arlie's uncle had his hands on the reins but his mind was far away, pulling up from memory all he knew about the most amazing bird that ever was. The road was bumpy and the wooden wagon seat was hard, but Arlie never noticed. His mouth was open, his eyes wide. He was listening with all his might. Maybe he knew, even then, that he was being given a destiny to fulfill.

On either side of the road were farm fields. It seemed to young Arlie that the fields had always been there. Farm fields were everywhere in Delaware County. But no, his uncle was saying, he could remember when there had been great forests of beech trees where those fields were now—trees with huge gray trunks like elephant skins and endless layers of broad leaves overhead. In autumn the ground beneath the trees was thick with beechnuts.

And those beechnuts brought the passenger pigeons. They were passengers, all right, always traveling. And in such numbers, such crowds, such vast flocks! They filled the sky, blanketing over the sun. Bright noon faded to a dim twilight when they came. There was never a more plentiful bird, and they all lived in North America, nowhere else. In 1860 there were at least three billion, maybe five billion, some guessed as many as 10 billion of them. (To understand these numbers, think about this: Nowadays, *all* the birds living in the U.S. put together total about six billion.)

In New England people had watched a flock fly overhead for a whole day. It was a mile wide and 320 miles long! That's like a single flock covering Interstate 71 all the way from Cleveland to Cincinnati—and farther! A flock in flight often formed into vast funnels, some said like tornadoes in slow motion. Others remembered that a flock in flight looked like a "rolling cylinder."

But no matter what the drama of the flock in motion, each passenger pigeon by itself was beautiful, with a gray-blue head, pink breast, red legs and wings of brown, gray and white. They were bigger than the pigeons you see today, up to 16 inches long. They were designed for power and speed, with strong chest muscles and pointed wings, and could fly 60 miles per hour, just under highway cruising speed.

Millions of passenger pigeons would swoop down, eat all the food they could find, then move on. Every day, every single bird ate about one cup of seeds, berries, fruits, nuts, worms and insects. Think of all those billions of cups of food, eaten every day! And, Arlie's uncle said, they loved beechnuts best of all. Arlie looked at the fields where the beech trees had been and thought about this.

He thought, too, about how wonderful it would have been to see those flocks. But his uncle had more to tell. The birds were wonderful, yes, but also terrible. The sound of the birds flying overhead made a roll of thunder that went on for hours. When a flock swooped down, the birds perched on every branch for miles around. When the branches were full, the pigeons would perch right on top of other pigeons—sometimes a dozen deep—until the weight of the bulky birds made the branches break and crash to the forest floor.

The noise of the crashing branches, on top of the croaks and coos, shrieks, warbles and "keek, keeek, KEEEEK" of the birds, was tremendously loud. People had to shout to be heard above the din. The endless racket nearly drove people mad.

"And don't forget, Arlie," his uncle said, "birds poop!" Beneath a flock in flight, the stinky stuff fell in heavy showers like snow or hail. Beneath a perched flock, the ground would be covered a thick, slick slime—sometimes piling up several feet deep!

And talk about greedy! If passenger pigeons were full of food when they saw something good to eat, they would throw up what was already in their stomachs to make room for more food. "Yuck!" Arlie thought, but he was fascinated.

He thought about all his uncle had said. He looked around the fields. There were a few birds flying here and there but no passenger pigeons. He had never seen a passenger pigeon. "Where are they now? What happened to them?" Arlie asked.

"Almost all gone," his uncle said, sadly. He explained that there were several reasons. For one thing, the birds had almost no fear of people. They were easy to shoot because they were forever flying about in search of food or nesting places. Hunters didn't even have to aim. They just shot up into the flocks, and the pigeons fell by the hundreds. The birds were cheap tasty food, and people stuffed pillows and quilts with their feathers.

For another thing, the pigeons needed large forests for shelter, and they didn't like to build their nests in open farmlands. And the most amazing thing was their need to live in a crowd. When the flocks shrank, the birds could no longer nest and breed comfortably. They could only live in huge flocks. They flew, ate, nested and did everything in huge numbers. They knew no other way. (In 1914, when Arlie was age 30, the last passenger pigeon died. Her name was Martha and she had lived in the Cincinnati Zoo.) From five billion to zero in 50 years! His uncle fell silent, thinking. Arlie thought, too. He thought long and hard, then and later.

Arlie grew and learned lots of stuff but never lost interest in birds. He read books about them and he watched how they lived. Arlie Schorger became known as an expert on birds. He never saw a flock of passenger pigeons, but he learned all he could about the bird. He became the director of the most famous bird-lovers' club of all, the Audubon Society.

Finally, when he was age 71, after a lifetime of study, he completed his great book, *The Passenger Pigeon*. His book made many people think and feel what Arlie had thought and felt when his uncle had told him that story so long ago. His book showed the world that we humans really can wipe out even the most numerous animals. Or we can decide to save them before it's too late.

The book has become a classic. Arlie Schorger's destiny was fulfilled.

To learn more...

Once There Was A Passenger Pigeon by Esther S. and Bernard L. Gordon (Henry Z. Walck, Inc., 1976)

Passenger Pigeon by Graham Coleman (The Extinct Species Collection, Gareth Stevens Publishing, 1996)

Passenger Pigeon by Susan Dudley Morrison (Silver Burdett Press, 1990)

For adult readers: *The Silent Sky: The Incredible Extinction of the Passenger Pigeon* by Allan W. Eckert (Lightning Source Inc., 2000)

Web sites

www.Audubon.org (National Audubon Society includes a special kids' page)

www.passengerpigeon.org/ (Passenger Pigeon Society)

www.enquirer.com/editions/2000/03/24/loc_passenger_pigeon.html (the last pigeon, Martha, with links)

www.usgennet.org/usa/wi/county/eauclaire/history/ourstory/vol1/pigeon.html (material from A.W. Schorger's *The Passenger Pigeon*)

www.ulala.org/P_Pigeon/George.html (story of a stuffed passenger pigeon named George)

8

The Wright Family's Robin

*Our next story is an example of historical fiction.
It's about a real Ohio family with two brothers who
became famous as the first to fly an airplane. It's all true,
except for the robin part, which may or may not have
happened. I hope the tale helps you understand how
Kate's strong personality influenced her family.*

Kate Wright meant to step outside for just a moment to shake out her dust rag. It was May, 1892, and she was very busy with spring cleaning. But the lilac bush caught her eye. Its blossoms were bursting like great purple volcanoes from a deep sea of green leaves. She stepped off the porch and into the yard and buried her face in them. Lips pressed tight, she pulled in a long, deep, delicious breath through her nose and then let out a long sigh.

Her mother Susan had loved lilacs. Three Mays earlier Kate had taken a vase of lilacs to her mother's bedside. Her mother had been so full of life and love that day and yet so weak and ill. Then, in mid-summer, she had died. They had known for a long time that she was failing, but it was still terribly hard. Oh, how the family missed her!

The family came to depend upon Kate. A month after the funeral Kate had gone away to visit friends for a week. Her father wrote to say, "But for you we should feel like we had no home." Kate knew her father and brothers needed her, and she believed it was her duty to make for them the best home she could. (At that time, people felt strongly about fulfilling their duties, and most thought it was women's duty to keep house.)

Kate sighed again and turned to go back inside. Then she saw it—a robin swooping under the porch roof, carrying a strand of straw. Kate crept closer. Right above the front door, of all places, the robin was building a nest. Kate could reach up and, with one swipe of the dust rag, that robin would have to find somewhere else to build her nest. But Kate didn't do it. Instead she went round to the back end of the fancy, filigreed wrap-around porch and entered through the side door.

Inside from behind a curtain, Kate watched the robin fly out and back, out and back, each time bringing bits of hay or grass. Kate was fascinated. It was so ordinary and yet so beautiful. So simple, yet lives depended upon it. The future depended upon it. No one made the robin do what she did. It was her duty.

Suddenly Kate heard shouts of laughter from down the street. It was her older brothers Wilbur and Orville back from one of their long bike rides. They were pulling up in front of the house and would soon be bounding up to the front door. Kate ran out the side door and went right up to them, waving both her hands.

"You can't use the front door!" she called out, frowning. "And you must be quiet!"

Wilbur was 25 and Orville was 21, but they were used to taking orders from their 18-year-old sister. She ran the house. So they fell silent and stood blinking at her. "A robin is building her nest above the front door," Kate whispered, pointing. "We'll be using the side door for a while."

"Oh, Kate! Come on!" the brothers complained. "Just shoo her away! That robin can find some other place for her nest, easy!"

"No!" Kate snapped back in a sharp whisper. The brothers knew she meant it. "She's going to nest there until her family has figured out how to fly!"

So for the next two months no one visiting at 7 Hawthorne Street, Dayton, Ohio, was allowed to come in or go out the front door. When church leaders came to see the Wright's father Reverend Milton Wright, Kate stood guard and waved them to the side door.

Neither was anyone allowed to sit on the porch. "Not until they learn to fly!" Kate insisted. Wilbur and Orville stayed clear, though they liked sitting out there. They were proud of that porch. They had built it themselves, the two brothers, together, from scratch. They'd made the black shutters, too, that hung on either side of every window in the two-story house. They'd built a lot of things together, even a printing press on which they printed their own newspaper. Many years later, Wilbur said, "From the time we were little, Orville and myself lived together, played together, worked together, and, in fact, thought together."

If Kate's brothers were good with their hands, it was because of their mother. When the boys wanted to know how to build something, they came to their mother. Susan had designed and built many things for the household. She could see how things were constructed and how they worked. She could make a picture in her head of how a thing should be and then set about making it. So could her boys. She'd even made toys for the children. She'd made a marvelous sled that was a family treasure.

Their father couldn't make things, but he loved to buy toys for his children. Once he'd brought home a toy helicopter. The Wright children never forgot the wonder they felt as they watched the little wooden toy fly up and bob against the ceiling.

But now it was bicycles. The brothers were crazy about them. Orville liked racing, but Wilbur liked long rides in the country where his legs could take him as far as he wanted to go and at his own speed. Gliding down a long hill was almost like flying. At such moments Orville and Wilbur felt that if they stretched out their arms, they might actually rise off their bicycle seats and soar through the air. What a thrill that would be!

If a bicycle was broken, the brothers could always figure out how to fix it. So they started a bicycle shop. Each weekday morning they'd get up, dress neatly in white shirts, vests and ties, eat the breakfast Kate made for them and set off for their bike shop. There they'd roll up their sleeves, put on their work aprons and get down to business. They loved tinkering with bicycles. Truth be told, they loved tinkering with anything mechanical.

Kate had a feeling that her brothers might do something great someday. Orville was shy but hopeful and full of ideas. Wilbur was more outgoing, more confident and always reading. Lately he'd been studying books about birds and how they fly, soar and can glide without beating their wings. Sometimes he wondered if maybe he and Orville could rig up a sort of a big kite that would... hmmmm.

One mid-summer day, Kate noticed that the robin's nest was empty. The bird had made a secure home for her family. She had fed them, taken care of them, given them what they needed. And that was why they were able to figure out how to fly. The robin had done her duty. Kate smiled.

To learn more...

The Wright Brothers: A Flying Start by Elizabeth MacLeod (Kids Can Press, 2002)

Taking Flight: The Story of the Wright Brothers by Stephen Krensky (Simon & Schuster Children's Book, 2001)

The Wright Brothers: Pioneers of American Aviation by Quentin Reynolds (Random House, 1997)

Robins by George K. Peck (Smart Apple Media, 1998) (in truth, robin fathers share parenting)

Web sites

www.activedayton.com/rec/content/services/travel/getaways/aviation_list.html
  (sites associated with the Wright family, Dayton, Ohio)

www.hfmgv.org (the original Wright Cycle Company, courtesy of the Henry Ford
  Museum & Greenfield Village, Dearborn, Michigan)

www.wright-brothers.org or www.first-to-fly.com (both sites access the virtual
  Wright Brothers Aeroplane Company & Museum of Pioneer Aviation and
  offer build-your-own-aircraft blueprints, plus links)

www.libraries.wright.edu/special/wright_brothers/dmc.html (The OhioLINK
  Digital Media Center offers fascinating original photographs, including the
  Hawthorn Street residence)

www.nasm.si.edu (the original 1903 *Flyer* preserved at the National Air and Space
  Museum, Smithsonian Institution, Washington, D.C.)

www.nps.gov/daav (The Dayton Aviation Heritage and National Historical Park,
  or call 937-225-7705)

www.nps.gov/wrbr (The Wright Brothers National Memorial at Kitty Hawk, N.C.)

www.wpafb.af.mil/museum (United States Air Force Museum, or call 937-255-3286)

9

Cy Gatton and the Chicken That Ate Lightning Bugs

*Cy Gatton was a beloved Richland County
storyteller, farmer and folk hero. I gathered up
his tall tales and wrote them down in my book
"Ripsnorting Whoppers." But I kept this one
aside to brighten your day.*

One summer evening Cy Gatton went out to his barn-yard. He pushed his hands under his belt, pursed his lips and sniffed in some cool, sweet air through his big, bushy walrus mustache. He was watching the lightning bugs rise out of the grass, little yellow blinks in the half-darkness. His old wrinkly face broke into a big, crinkly smile. He loved lightning bugs. So pretty. You don't think about them all winter long and then summer comes. And one night—there they are!

Then he saw that he wasn't the only one watching the lightning bugs. His chicken was watching them, too!

Then he saw that she wasn't just watching them. She was chasing them!

Then he saw that she wasn't just chasing them. She was eating them! Eee-yoooo!

Cy never heard of a chicken eating lightning bugs! In fact, it was just about the most unheard of thing he'd ever heard of! But suddenly it came to him that this chicken might be on to a good thing! "If this chicken eats lightning bugs," he said, "it'll save us money on chicken feed! Lightning bugs are free!"

He yelled to his kids. "Come on out and catch some lightning bugs!" And Earl and Nell Gatton came out of the house quick. They ran round the barnyard, catching the lightning bugs in glass jars. Then they poured all the lightning bugs they had caught into a big bowl. They set the bowl down in front of the chicken.

There must have been a hundred lightning bugs in that bowl, easy. She chased down and ate down every last one of them. Then she burped a funny little chicken burp. "Urp!" she said.

Then she turned and went inside her chicken coop, a little house where she had her nest. And Cy and the kids went inside the Gatton farmhouse and ate supper. Cy told a few of his famous tall tales to the kids, and then the family all went to bed.

In the middle of the night, Cy woke up, sudden-like. Cy wondered what had made him wake up. Something was troubling him. Then he knew. He was worrying about that chicken. Would she be all right? Maybe they shouldn't have given her so many bugs.

He got out of his bed and went to the window. He pulled aside the curtain. A few stars peeked through the pitch-black leaves of the shade trees around Cy's house.

Cy looked across the dark barnyard. He could just make out the chicken coop. He half-thought he might see a weird yellow glow coming out of that chicken coop. But there was no weird yellow glow. Everything seemed normal.

Still, Cy was worried. He pulled on his pants, and he went downstairs and outside. The dusty ground felt soft and cool under his bare feet as he crossed the barnyard. He slowly pushed open the door of the chicken coop. The rusty hinges made a weird, scraping "Eeeeeeeee."

There was the chicken, sitting on her nest. He half-thought he might see a weird yellow glow coming out of her eyes. But there was no weird yellow glow.

Everything seemed okay.

"Well," he said out loud, "I guess I've come out here for nothing."

Then he supposed he might as well look in her nest, the way he did first thing every morning. That's what you do on a farm, first thing every morning. You look in the chicken's nest.

So he shooshed her aside, just the way he always did. He looked in her nest. And that was when he come to find that his chicken, after eating *all* those lightning bugs, had

laid

a

dozen

ELECTRIC LIGHT BULBS!

To learn more...

Ripsnorting Whoppers: Humor from the American Heartland, by Rick Sowash
    (Gabriel's Horn Publishing Company, 1994)
Fireflies by Janet Halfmann (Smart Apple Media, 1999)
Fireflies by Sally M. Walker (Early Bird Nature Books, Lerner Publications
    Company, 2001)

Web sites
www.sowash.com/RipWhop.html (information about Cy Gatton)
www.americanfolklore.net/folktales (tall tales from each state)
www.storycraft.com (Kids' Storytelling Club)
www.storynet.org (provides useful links)
http://lcweb.loc.gov/folklife (American Folklife Center offers a teacher's guide)
www.eosdev.com/Nature/fireflies.htm (useful links, including a link to "Summer
    Science: Firefly Babies Advertise Their Bitter Taste" that explains why nobody
    should eat fireflies—they're very bitter)

10

American Bald Eagles

Did you ever wonder how we know so much about wild animals and how they hunt, mate and raise their young? We know because someone went to a lot of trouble to observe them. Here's the story of a man who went to an awful lot of trouble.

Lightning struck with the hiss of doom. Thunder broke so near that Charles Shipman's teeth rattled. The afternoon storm spit fire and spouted rain. Scary enough for someone safe and dry at home, peeking out a window, but Charles was weathering this storm inside a tent on a platform atop an eight-story steel tower. The storm lashed the forest below, stripping off leaves.

Then the raindrops turned to hailstones, thumping the canvas walls of the tent. The branches of a nearby tree beat upon the tower. The platform leaned and swayed, groaning at every blast. Charles clung to the floor. If the tower blew over, he'd be killed for sure.

Suddenly, the tent flap ripped open, and he caught a glimpse of the top of a neighboring tree. It was swaying even more than the tower, but the mother eagle that had made her nest there had not flown to safety. Instead, she was braving the hailstones, guarding her young.

Even the worst storm is soon over. The wind died, the rain slowed, the thunder grew distant. Fifteen minutes later sunlight made everything glisten. The tower was still standing, Charles was still at his post and the bald eagle was at hers.

Charles Shipman, amateur naturalist, was determined to learn all he could about bald eagles, no matter what. The bird had been America's national symbol since 1782, but little was known about it in 1925 when Shipman first climbed the steel tower. No one had ever really studied the eagles and the birds were badly misunderstood. People said they sometimes carried off chickens, sheep, calves, even babies! Many bald eagles were shot. Their numbers fell.

Knowledge of the national bird was much needed, but eagles

were almost impossible to study. No human could get close enough to observe them without scaring them off.

Then a Cleveland professor named Dr. Francis Herrick had an idea: since eagles use and expand the same nest year after year, build a steel tower near a nest. Top it with a platform, pitch a tent on it, live there and make notes. The birds could be watched and photographed and their family life followed through the seasons over several years. If he could prove his hunch that bald eagles did not eat farm animals but mostly fish and rats, then perhaps laws could be passed to protect the bird. But the professor couldn't spend months in a tower. He was needed in the classroom. So he found a willing fellow naturalist–Charles–to do the job.

The tower was built next to an old hickory tree that held one of the largest bird nests in America. This amazing nest was located a mile south of Lake Erie near Vermilion. It was 12-feet tall, 8-feet wide and weighed 4,000 pounds, about the size of two pick-up trucks stacked on top of each other. Eagles had used it for 36 years. It seemed perfect.

But then in March, 1925, a storm blew down the tree with the nest. The eagles didn't seem too discouraged by this setback, for they were soon building a new nest in a red oak nearby. So the next winter the naturalists built a new steel tower. It was 4-feet square and 81-feet high, just a little higher than the eagle's nest.

Charles arrived early and passed each day keeping track of all he saw. He brought along a camp stool, binoculars, camera, thermometer, notebooks, sandwiches and a thermos of coffee. Lake Erie gleamed in the north. Fields, farms and forest stretched out in the other directions.

He enjoyed writing in his notebooks about "mornings among

the treetops before the coming of the sun...to know the woods as the birds see it...the rising sun, with shreds of clouds like hand-maidens of brilliant color...the tree trunks and the earth below in purples and grays...but over there, outlined against the sky—the eagle!" He observed his lofty neighbors, "three beautiful white eaglets, bright-eyed and cute...what a joy it was to look into one of those great birds' nests and see the newly hatched fluffs of down!"

He was the first naturalist to observe many things, including the activity in the eagle nursery. He saw how the eaglet's downy baby-feathers dropped away as they grew. The tiny feathers blew about the nest and even blew into his tent. He saw the babies awake, stretch, even yawn. He saw them play together, jumping on a stick, sinking in their talons, trying to flap into the air while carrying it. Charles wrote to his daughter, "My dear little Gretta: Up in the air! I am writing this from inside the tent way up on the top of the tower, and the old eagle sits a short way over in a tree. Baby Eagle is crawling around on its feet and wings. It uses its wings for front legs like a little kitten."

But there were more setbacks. A storm struck and the next day Charles was shocked to find the old red oak topless and the great nest destroyed. He found the dead bodies of the little eaglets and saw "the old eagles...sitting side by side and looking thin and gaunt, soaking wet." He was heartbroken.

The next year the researchers found a nest near Geneva and built another tower. All went well until one day when the eagles simply vanished. Senselessly, someone had climbed the tree and pulled the nest over, destroying the eggs.

Despite these setbacks, Professor Herrick and his team still didn't give up. They found another nest in a great ash tree near

Vermilion, 86 feet off the ground. The following spring Charles was back in the tower, writing in his notebooks.

"A perfect day with sailing clouds...across the blue background you saw [the eagle] coming...with a great sweep she poised over the nest...and in one talon was a beautiful, shining fish. There in the air she held and swayed for fully five seconds, until the breeze lulled—whereupon she dropped down to those eager white babies...it was the most spectacular sight and always thrilling to me." The fish, if still alive, would flip and flop as the eaglets practiced their hunting skills.

Another time he watched as "for an hour she combed feather after feather with her beak...then she would smooth all down with her head...each great white feather in the tail must be combed in the same way."

Summer came and he suffered through terrible heat up to 104° F. Stripped to his undershorts, he noted the mother standing with her wings slightly lowered, shading her babies from the sun.

Wonders filled his days. "A great rainbow, one end resting on the lake, rising and arching until it merged in the gray mists." He watched as the scene changed. "The lake was utterly blue, the horizon cut like a knife...then, like a mirage in the sky, I could see the islands miles to the west off Sandusky Bay."

On another day "the lake was a marvel of blue water ridged with whitecaps which chased each other off to the north in endless procession." And always there were the eagles. "Great tumbling rolling globes of clouds against an exquisite blue, with the eagle...sailing across the front of the clouds and the cobalt spaces in between."

One foggy morning he "found all nature moist and veiled in

mist, an eerie, uncanny morning. I seemed to leave earth behind and ascend into another world." The nest was only a ghostly outline, but he could hear the eagle calling nearby.

He watched the first flights of the eaglets. They nearly fell to the ground but then circled, pumping hard to return to the nest to rest and sleep. "Less and less did they return," he noted. "More and more the open woods and the shores of Lake Erie became [their] home."

After five years of watching eagles, Professor Herrick and Charles Shipman shared with others all they had learned. In 1940 their years of dedication paid off. Congress passed the Bald Eagle Act to protect the bird. A pair of determined Ohioans had helped save the American Bald Eagle.

To learn more...
The Bald Eagle by Steve Potts (Wildlife of North America, Capstone Press, 1998)
Amazing Bald Eaglet by Barbara Birenbaum (Pear Tree, 1999)
Bald Eagles (Really Wild Life of Birds of Prey) by Doug Wechsler (Powerkids Press, 2001)
Fly Eagle Fly by Sally Moorer and James Rogers (Insight Publishing Company, 2001) includes an interactive CD
Bald Eagles: Majesty in Motion by John L. Eliot (National Geographic Magazine, July 2002)

Web sites
http://midwest.fws.gov/ottawa (visit Ottawa National Wildlife Refuge to see bald eagles and other migratory birds, or telephone 419-898-0014)
nerrs.noaa.gov/OldWomanCreek (visit Old Woman Creek National Estuary to see eagle nests, or telephone 419-433-4601)
www.eagles.org (American Eagle Foundation, with nesting cam)
www.birds-of-prey.org (The Birds of Prey Foundation offers useful links)
http://biology.boisestate.edu/raptor (Raptor Research Foundation)
www.Audubon.org (National Audubon Society includes a special kids' page)

Louis Bromfield's
Remarkable Pig

Just a few rolling ridges northeast of Cy Gatton's farm is Malabar Farm. That's where Louis Bromfield lived, wrote and experimented with better farming methods. Louis loved and admired his animals—and one very smart pig in particular.

Louis Bromfield shook his head in wonder as he stared at one of his pigs. He pushed his hand across his craggy face and rubbed his brown butch haircut. His eyebrows waggled and his big, crooked teeth showed as he smiled a puzzled smile. "Pig," he thought, "you are, just now, the biggest mystery at Malabar Farm."

Malabar Farm in Richland County, Ohio, was one of the most famous farms in America during the middle of the twentieth century. It was Louis Bromfield's farm and Louis Bromfield was famous. He was a best-selling author. His best-selling books won prizes and were made into movies starring famous actors of the day. (For example, he wrote the screenplay for Mae West's first film "Night After Night.") Many of his Hollywood friends visited Malabar Farm, including James Cagney, Errol Flynn and Shirley Temple.

Louis had served in World War I and afterwards stayed on in France for more than 20 years. He visited many countries, but he became homesick for the rolling hills of Richland County where the land was rich and where he had been born.

So he came back to Ohio. He bought four little neighboring worn-out farms in the south of the county and put them together into one big farm. He called it Malabar Farm after a region of southern India. He thought those two places were the most beautiful in the world: Malabar in India and Richland County in Ohio. (Today Malabar Farm is one of Ohio's most popular state parks.)

Louis then set to work to heal the worn-out land. He'd always loved and studied plants and animals. In Paris he had designed and managed his own flower gardens and became well known. When he got together with other American writers who lived in France, like Gertrude Stein and Ernest Hemingway, they rarely discussed books. Instead the talk was about gardening, which Louis loved far more than writing.

So Louis farmed and grew crops in Ohio. He plowed some of them under to enrich the tired soil. He changed the crops around, from field to field, growing corn one year and hay the next, letting the soil rest and recover. All sorts of animals lived at the farm. He got good and dirty (stinky, too) spreading their manure across the fields. He loved it. Louis loved everything about being a farmer.

Then he wrote books about his farm. They weren't storybooks to be made into movies. They were books that told other farmers how to save their soil, sharing the joys and struggles that came to someone living close to land, plants and animals. In one of those books, *Animals and Other People,* he told about the puzzling pig.

He seemed like an ordinary pig. He looked just like the other 200 pigs in Malabar Farm's fenced-in 10-acre pig lot. The puzzling thing was that every day, week after week, this pig escaped the pig lot. Again and again he was found in the cornfield next to the pig lot, stuffing himself with dozens of ears of plump, sweet corn.

Now, the pig lot was completely surrounded by a pig-proof fence. And none of the other 199 pigs ever escaped. Only this one.

Was the pig flying over the fence when no one was looking? You've heard the sayings: "When pigs have wings!" or "When pigs fly!" It's a way Ohioans have of saying that something is impossible. "Oh sure, I'll believe *that* when pigs have wings!"

After weeks of chasing the pig around the cornfield and rustling him back into the pig lot, Louis was just about ready to believe that this pig really could fly.

Then one day Louis happened to be near the pig lot when he

saw something he could scarcely believe. He saw the pig climbing the fence!

The openings at the bottom of the fence were too small for even the smallest piglet to wriggle through. The openings were larger toward the top of the fence. Of all the pigs in the field, only this one pig seemed to have discovered this. As Louis watched in amazement, the corn-loving pig oomphed his front hooves high enough to reach an opening that was big enough for him to get through. When he'd gotten his head and piggy armpits through, he kicked his hind legs against the ground over and over until he just managed to flop through to the other side. Then he scrambled headlong for the corn!

Just as some people are smarter than others, so some pigs are smarter than others. Louis knew that. He loved and admired all his animals, but now he loved and admired this pig most of all. Louis loved and admired that pig so much that he didn't tell any of the other farm workers that he'd discovered the pig's secret escape plan. He just let the pig enjoy his daily adventure.

But the free lunch didn't last forever. The pig got fatter and fatter, eating all that sweet corn. He grew larger and heavier. Finally, he could no longer hoist his bulk up to the larger openings and slip through. He tried but always fell back with a thud in the soft rich mud of his Richland County pig lot. At length he had to be content with the pig slops that were good enough for the other 199 porkers.

I like to think that the pig never forgot those wild adventures of his youth, when, by a combination of brain power and determination, he alone, of all the pigs, managed to flip himself through the fence and on to greener pastures.

To learn more...
Pigs by Sara Swan Miller (A True Book, Children's Press, 2000)
Life on a Pig Farm by Judy Wolfman (Carolrhoda Books, Inc., 1998)
Pig Tales by Kate Tym (Element Books Inc., 1999)

Web sites
www.malabarfarm.org (information about Louis Bromfield's career and travels, the Bogart/Bacall wedding at the farm, a kids' page and travel directions, or call 419-892-2784)
http://netvet.wustl.edu/pigs.htm (links to everything porcine)
www.northcanton.sparcc.org/~greentown/farmunit.htm (a fun school web site)
www.fourhcouncil.edu (4H Clubs)
www.kerala.gov.in/ (photographs of India's Malabar coast, today in Kerala)
www.localharvest.org (discover other organic farms in Ohio)

Just for fun
www.pigsonparade.org (Seattle's painted street pigs)
www.piggingassnppsa.com/about.htm (a completely different type of smart pig)

12

Muskrat Attack —
An Amish Story

Amish folks are different. They do things their own way. Our next story involves a boy of the Amish faith, a very strange muskrat and a dangerous disease, rabies.

Later, when it was all over, the principal said, "Kids get bit by a lot of things on the way to school—dogs, cats—but I'd never heard of anyone being bit by a muskrat!"

It all started when Abe Yoder set off for school one October morning not long ago. October shows off Ohio: orange, red, yellow, purple, gold—a flood of color spills across the hills and the sky is never bluer. Three weeks later it's all gone. Bare black branches hang in the fog like dead claws. If October is color, November is death.

But it was still bright October on this particular morning in Holmes County, Ohio. The maples still had all their leaves. They made a fine picture, those maples, cuddling up to the big white barn and the two-story white farmhouse where Abe's family lived. The sun was just breaking through the morning mist as Abe began the half-mile walk down the farm lane to where the school bus stopped.

A typical Ohio farm scene, you imagine. But look more closely. No telephone wires or electric wires run to the house from power lines along the county road. Dozens of plain dark dresses and pants hang from the clotheslines in the yard. A buggy can be seen through the open barn door but no automobiles or tractors. In the surrounding fields, bearded men dressed in dark blue are using farm equipment drawn by horses.

The Yoders are Amish. That day, and every day, Abe wore a straw hat. His jacket had hooks and eyes—no buttons. His trousers were held up by suspenders—no belt. His lunch pail was filled with homemade foods his mother had prepared from scratch—no junk food there.

Abe was the youngest Yoder. Hundreds of times his eight

older brothers and sisters had walked that quiet farm lane to the bus stop. Nothing had ever happened to them. Today would be different.

Schooling is important to most Amish. It's where they learn English, for one thing, so they can speak to other Americans. Among themselves many Amish speak only a form of German. At school they learn reading and math so that some day they can manage their family's farming business. Some Amish children go to all-Amish schools. Some, like the Yoder children, attend public schools. Amish folk are not exactly alike in all ways, but usually their children leave school after the eighth grade.

The Amish are not against education or telephones or buttons or tractors. They simply believe that these get in the way of more important things, like their relationship to God, their family and their community. Think how often your own family life is interrupted by the telephone and maybe you'll begin to see, at least partly, why the Amish have made these choices.

Back to Abe. The Yoder farm lane crosses a bridge over a little stream that flows into Sugar Creek. Abe was nearing this bridge when something out of the corner of his eye caught his full attention. Something was coming on with shiny fur, short ears, and short legs and it was moving fast. It was a muskrat, the biggest of all rats, big as a cat. And it was charging straight at him. Abe jumped back but the animal sprang at his leg and bit down hard with his sharp teeth. Abe felt a burst of hot pain just above the ankle. Too late, Abe screamed and swung his lunch pail at the critter. It turned and bolted off under the bridge. Its musky smell lingered behind.

Abe didn't know what to do. His leg was hurting badly. He

thought about limping back home but just then the school bus came into sight. Abe grabbed his bleeding leg and lurched to the bus stop. As he struggled aboard, the bus driver wanted to know what was wrong. "A muskrat bit me," Abe replied. The bus driver just stared at him in disbelief.

On the bus Abe tried to forget the pain by watching the passing farms, rich with the autumn harvest. He also thought about what had happened. Abe knew muskrats. He and his brothers had trapped them many times, skinned them and sold the fur. It wasn't natural for a muskrat to ambush a human being. Something was wrong.

At Mount Hope Elementary School Abe told his teacher and then the principal about the attack. Right away they cleaned the bite and put medicine on it. The principal phoned a doctor, the health department, the game warden, and the county extension agent. None of them had ever heard of a muskrat biting a human. The bite itself was nothing much to worry about. What they all feared was rabies.

Rabies is a disease caused by a virus in the spit of an infected animal. It attacks the central nervous system and finally the brain. Without treatment rabies almost always causes death. Any warm-blooded animal can carry rabies, but raccoons are the most common carriers, followed by skunks, bats and foxes.

The game warden brought Abe home from school that day. He poked around the muskrat's nest but could find no clues to show if the animal had rabies or not.

That night the Yoders discussed and prayed about what to do for Abe. At that time rabies shots cost about $1,000, a lot of money for a large farm family. The shots had to be given often and over a period of several weeks. It would be difficult for the family to get Abe back and forth to the doctor so many times. Did the muskrat actually have rabies?

Animals with rabies behave strangely and do unexpected things. Sometimes they walk slowly as if they're dizzy or drunk. Sometimes a nighttime animal, such as a raccoon, will come out in broad daylight.

However, this muskrat had come out at dawn and was very fast. That seemed normal enough. Maybe it was just startled or defending its young. Still, a handful of Americans die tragically of rabies each year. Of course, the Yoders loved Abe dearly and could not bear to think of losing him. What to do? Again, they prayed and asked God to guide them. Then they decided Abe would not get the shots.

The days passed slowly and anxiously. The leaves fell from the trees as the dark and death of November set in. Abe wondered if, like the leaves, he would also soon die. The bite healed but Abe knew his family was still watching him, fearing to see tiredness, fever, headache—the first signs of rabies. If he showed no symptoms after a month, he would be all right.

The Yoders waited and they prayed. Each morning Abe awoke feeling just fine. But it wasn't until Thanksgiving Day that the family really knew for sure that Abe was going to be okay. Thanksgiving was mighty joyful that year on the Yoder farm.

To learn more...

Amish Horses by Richard Ammon, illustrated by Pamela Patrick (Simon & Schuster Children's, 2001)

An Amish Christmas by Richard Ammon, illustrated by Pamela Patrick (Simon & Schuster Children's, 2000)

Amish Home by Raymond Bial (Houghton Mifflin Company, 1995)

The Amish (video) Heritage Productions (Gateway Films, 2000) a PBS broadcast

The Plain People of Pennsylvania by Jerry Irwin (National Geographic Magazine, April 1984)

Rodents of the World by David Alderton (Facts on File, 1996)

Rabies by Elaine Landau (Lodestar Books, 1993)

Web sites

www.amish.net (information and links to Amish communities nation-wide)

www.visitamishcountry.com (Holmes County tourist information)

www.amish-heartland.com (links and a message board)

http://my.net-link.net/~vaneselk/muskrat/home.htm (everything about muskrats, including recipes!)

www.cdc.gov/ncidod/dvrd/rabies (Centers for Disease Control and Prevention offers a kids' page about rabies)

13

The Wilds

A visit to The Wilds will make your eyes pop. It did ours. My wife and I blinked in amazement. The landscape and creatures are so unexpected that I just had to joke, "Jo-Jo, I don't think we're in Ohio anymore..."

L aura and Jenna could hardly see each other's faces. Only a dim glimmer of starlight sifted through the tall prairie grass and they had no flashlights. Each cousin wondered what the other was thinking. They weren't exactly scared. And they certainly weren't wishing they were safe back home in Columbus, Ohio. Still, the weirdness of the moment cast a definite spell. The wild calling of red-crowned cranes—birds almost as tall as the cousins—was strange enough by day. At night the cries sounded fiercely human, like a band of Zulu warriors on the attack.

The cries of the cranes also reached the ears of a rhinoceros herd, motionless in the dark less than a mile from the two girls. Giraffes, lost against the black branches of a nearby tree, heard the calls as did zebras, camels and a herd of Cape buffalo. And a family of onagers, the fastest horse-like creatures on earth (42 miles per hour) pricked their ears forward at the sound. So did the little Przewalski's wild horses, who share an ancestor common to all modern horses. (These are the stocky horses that were hunted by cave men 35,000 years ago and painted on walls deep inside the caves of France.)

And many other animals in the surrounding grasslands, wetlands and clumps of trees heard the cranes that night. None of them took much notice. They just kept on grazing or sleeping. The cries of the cranes were as common to those creatures as grass, water and the stars.

Where do you suppose this scene took place? Africa? India? Guess again. Something like it happens almost every night in Muskingum County, Ohio, at a place called The Wilds. Laura and Jenna were on a night hike, part of one of the most amazing summer camp adventures a kid can have.

Nearly 10,000 acres make up the lands called The Wilds. Seventy-five years ago it was typical Ohio farmland, with rolling cornfields. The only herds were cows and sheep. Then the land was bought by mining companies, and strip mines were dug across the land, huge holes, miles wide. The guts of the earth were opened up to the sky. But Ohio needed the coal that lay in the earth.

A vast amount of dirt had to be moved. A lot of the work was done by a steam shovel called "Big Muskie," one of the most amazing machines ever built. Big Muskie was not only the world's largest earth-moving machine, it was the world's largest land vehicle. Big Muskie weighed 27 million pounds and was wide enough to straddle an eight-lane highway. Big Muskie's boom was 300 feet long. The bucket of the shovel could lift a two-story house, easy. You can still see Big Muskie's bucket at McConnelsville.

You could almost call Big Muskie an animal—an Amazing Animal of Ohio—because the machine could actually walk! It had no wheels. It lumbered along on hydraulic feet at a snail's pace of about 20 inches a minute. Year in, year out, Big Muskie gouged the earth, set aside the dirt, took out the coal. Then, when the coal was gone, Big Muskie closed up the holes and put the dirt back where it had been. Grass was planted. This is called reclaiming the land.

An open strip mine is not a pretty thing, but land that has been reclaimed can be very beautiful. True, trees don't seem to grow as well or as tall on reclaimed land. No one knows quite why. But water gathers in the valleys and there are long graceful grassy hills, with shapes unlike other hills in Ohio. The Wilds looks like the veld, the wide rolling grassy plains of southern Africa.

American Electric Power owned the land. When their work

was done, they donated it to The Wilds. The animals that live at The Wilds come from zoos all over America. Living in the open is natural for animals. Scientists come to The Wilds to study how the animals behave when they are not enclosed as they would be in zoos.

The purpose of The Wilds is to give these animals the space, protection and care they need—and to help Ohioans learn about animals, nature and conservation. Visitors can board a bus for a six-mile safari tour, complete with a picture book of the animals and a guide to explain what is seen.

What seem like big gray rocks in the distance turn out to be a rhino herd when the bus brings you near. You think you're looking at an ordinary little forest? Then a tree moves in a way that trees don't usually move. You realize it's not a tree. It's a giraffe, 17 feet tall. The guide tells you to watch carefully as they swallow their cud and then bring it back up. You can actually see the lump of cud rippling up and down inside the giraffe's neck.

If you want to learn more, the summer camp program is the way to go. The campers get the bus tour, but then they get to ride in the feed-truck. In the stalls where the animals are cared for and sheltered in the winter, Laura stroked a rhino and fed him a banana. Jenna held out an apple to a giraffe and got slimed by the creature's long, dark purple-blue tongue. "At first Jenna was grossed out," Laura said, "but then she thought it was kind of cool!"

The night walks through the prairie grass may seem dangerous with so many wild animals roaming free. But the cousins weren't ever really scared. There are miles of big, electric fences and heavy-duty electronic gates to contain the animals. It reminds you of movies you've seen. One camper called the place Giraffe-ick Park.

The people who run The Wilds dream big. They plan to expand the prairie and introduce bison, moose and maybe elk. Such hooved animals turn the prairie sod, and their dung fertilizes the grass. Herds are part of what makes a prairie.

And there are yet bigger dreams that include Siberian tigers, Asian bears and African wild dogs. The Wilds has enough land for those animals to roam freely and form social groups. There's even talk of bringing a herd of Asian elephants to The Wilds someday.

I think Laura summed it up: awesome.

To learn more...
(Your library has many books about the giraffe, rhinoceros, bison, tiger and bear.)
24 Hours in a Game Reserve by Barrie Watts (Franklin Watts, 1991)
Przewalski's Horse by Charlotte Wilcox (Capstone Press, 1997)
Mystery of Lascaux Cave by Dorothy Hinshaw Patent (Benchmark Books, 1999)
Animal Rescue: The Best Job There Is by Susan E. Goodman (Simon & Schuster Books for Young Readers, 2000)

Web sites
www.thewilds.org (to arrange a visit to The Wilds, or call 740-638-5030)
www.thewildones.org/Animals/redcrown.html (red-crowned cranes)
www.arabianwildlife.com/archive/vol1.2/onager.htm (onagers)
www.treemail.nl/takh (foundation dedicated to save Przewalski's horse)
http://little-mountain.com/bigmuskie (photographs and links for Big Muskie)
http://kidtravels.com/goalelementary.htm (GOAL's First Place essay about Big Muskie)

www.ohiosaf.org/siteprep.htm (planting trees on reclaimed strip mines in Ohio)
http://web.utk.edu/~nolt/radio/stripmn.htm (for another view of strip mining)
http://nature-wildlife.com/gir007.html (giraffe information and images)
www.fonz.org/zoogoer/zg1996/zggiraf.htm (all about giraffes)
http://news.bbc.co.uk/2/hi/sci/tech/393622.stm (about giraffe tongues)

14

Hellbender

*When you're known as a teller of tall tales
as I am, it can be difficult to get people to believe you
when you're telling the truth. I've often had
that problem when telling people
about the hellbender.*

When people ask me what I think is the most amazing animal of Ohio, I answer truthfully. I look them in the eye and say, "The hellbender." Right away, they think I'm kidding. It sounds like a ripsnorting monster found only in books of tall tales.

Well, the hellbender *is* monstrous to behold. In fact, it's by far the ugliest animal I've ever seen. But it is a really-oh, truly-oh creature that actually does live here in the Buckeye State.

Convinced at last that I'm not joking, people next want to know how the beast got its name. No one knows for sure. The dictionary says that the word is a slang term for someone who is exceedingly reckless or extreme. Experts guess that the creature got its official name because of its extreme ugliness. But it has had a lot of other names down through the years, including devil dog, mud puppy, mud lizard, mud devil, land pike, water dog, water puppy and tweeg. Tweeg, you say? That's right. Tweeg. I tell you, I'm *not* making this up!

What's so ugly about it? What does it look like? Well, let me tell you a little story. It's a true story and I know our two heroes aren't the only ones to have met a hellbender. It's probably happened hundreds of times around the state of Ohio. This time it happened where the Scioto River flows into the Ohio at Portsmouth, not far from the marina at Shawnee State Park, in Scioto County.

Early one morning two buddies named Harliss and Delbert set out to do some fishing there at Shawnee. They planned to spend the whole day casting off from Delbert's rowboat and brought along one of those medium-size coolers with enough ice to chill their sandwiches, pickles and drinks. They fished side by side for a couple of hours, enjoyed some lunch, but didn't have much luck.

Then Harliss thought maybe he'd do better fishing in the shade along the riverbank, so Delbert rowed in and dropped him off. Lazily, the boat drifted downstream about a half mile or so.

Suddenly Delbert was aware that something very large and camouflaged was creeping about below his boat. It was incredibly hideous with folds of wrinkly skin and about as long as Delbert's leg. But Delbert happened to be one of the few Ohioans who had actually seen one of these shy creatures before. He knew right off that he was looking at a hellbender. He shuddered as he stared at it. It was loathsome to look at as it clambered over the rocks in the riverbed.

Then a sly smile crept across Delbert's face. An idea had come to him. If he could just catch that creature, he could play a heck of a joke on Harliss. Disgusted by the creature's wild hideousness, he nevertheless managed to snag it in his largest net. As he hauled it on board, it struggled and dripped ropes of mucus. It was over two feet long and heavier than he'd expected. Taking care not to slime himself by touching the varmint, he tipped it out of his net and aimed it straight into the cooler, right on top of the leftovers from lunch. He flipped down the lid, dipped oars and rowed back to Harliss, trying to keep a straight face. This was going to be so great!

By the way, do you know how many state parks, like Shawnee State Park, there are in Ohio? How many would you guess? Twenty? Thirty? Try *seventy-three*! Is that amazing or what? After the new park opens on Middle Bass Island, there will be seventy-four! And they're wonderful parks! Full of all sorts of interesting things and recognized nationally! Ohio was the first state to win the National

Gold Medal Award for the best state park system. The award is given by the National Sporting Goods Manufacturers, and Ohio won it, two years in a row! Not only that but our parks are also tops in attendance nationally. That's right! More people visit Ohio state parks than visit any other state parks.

But, what's this? You want me to get back to the two fishermen? Oh, sorry, I got off the subject.

Well, when Delbert rowed up, Harliss was mighty glad to get back in the boat. He still hadn't caught anything and the mosquitoes were fierce along the shady banks. Delbert rowed back out onto the current. They fished some more. The sun rose. The afternoon got hotter and hotter. Delbert waited.

Finally, Harliss said, "I'm getting thirsty." He reached behind, felt for the cooler, flipped the latch and stuck his hand in. Puzzled, he twisted around to look and *screamed* at the top of his lungs! Not only that, but he leapt to his feet, waving his arms and dancing with terror. He lost his balance and toppled over backwards, right out of the boat and—splash!—into the river.

Delbert laughed so hard, he about split. But eventually he got Harliss back in the boat, especially easy after he threatened to tip the hellbender back into the river near where Harliss was treading water. He explained that the thing in the cooler was a just a little old hellbender. "The thing's a lot like you, Harliss, hideous to look at but harmless after all." And he told how it came to be in the cooler.

Now, just what *are* hellbenders, whether you find them in a river or a lunch cooler? Hellbenders are this hemisphere's largest salamander. They have a protective covering of mucus which makes them look like a giant lizard that just crawled out of a barrel of rubber cement. They're usually grayish brown, though sometimes they're entirely black. They breathe entirely through their skin, especially the loose flaps of thick wrinkles that run along their sides. They have flat heads, short stout legs, a long slimy tail, and very small beady eyes.

Daytime they stay mostly under large slabs of rock on the bottoms of rivers. After dark they slide along in search of food—mostly crayfish and frogs.

The males see to the nest. Every September they dig a hole under a rock and get a female to come inside with them. Females lay two long strings of about 300 eggs. The pair slowly sways within the nest, mixing fluid amid the eggs. Males then drive the females out and stay within the nest. They safeguard the eggs until hatching takes place in November. After five to seven years hellbenders are fully grown. They can live up to 30 years.

Hellbenders like clean, swift running streams and rivers with plenty of riffle areas (which stir oxygen into the water) and large flat rocks to use for cover and nesting sites.

Not much else is known about these shy and mysterious creatures. Their numbers seem to be dropping. Why? You can tick off the main reasons: pollution; dams, which remove the riffles; and floods of muddy runoff from farms and construction sites. But there is one more. Fishermen sometimes catch hellbenders accidentally. Probably because hellbenders are so ugly, they are sometimes thought to be poisonous. Senselessly, sportsmen sometimes kill these gentle giants.

Fishermen should understand that these huge salamanders are not in the least harmful or dangerous, ugly though they may be. So when Delbert played his joke on Harliss, he was really just trying to educate him. At least that's what Delbert tried to tell Harliss. But I don't think Harliss was ever completely convinced.

I never heard how, but I'll bet Harliss got even with Delbert. Somehow or other, sooner or later.

To learn more...

General guides that include hellbender information and photographs;

Salamanders: Secret, Silent Lives by Sara Swan Miller (Franklin Watts, 1999)

Amazing Amphibians by Sara Swan Miller (Franklin Watts, 2001)

Amphibians by Dr. Barry Clarke (Eyewitness Books, Alfred A. Knopf, 1993)

Web sites

www.hellbenders.sanwalddesigns.com (web page of J. Humphries—Ohio's hellbender guru)

www.marshall.edu/herp/hellbender/hellphotos.htm (photographs)

http://frenchcreek.alleg.edu/Hellbender.html (hellbenders in Pennsylvania)

15

Zebra Mussels

When I was a young reader, I loved science fiction.
When I researched zebra mussels for this book,
I felt a science fiction–type of story emerging.
After a while, I thought, why fight it?
Next stop, the twilight zone . . .

*(Imagine low, pulsating music, scary as it swells and recedes.
Now read the first paragraph in a deep, husky, movie-preview voice.)*

They came from afar. Aliens, ruthless invaders in vast hordes. The Zeebs...hideous, faceless creatures. No arms, no legs, no heads. Their tender flesh protected by smooth, rock-hard, glistening armor. Dark brown, the color of dried blood, slashed with stripes of tan and white, like the uniforms of an evil empire. Headlines screamed dire warnings, but the humans, helpless and unprepared, were powerless to stop them. The aliens used no weapons. No laser swords, no laser beams. They had little need of such things. Instead, they seized control of the one thing without which no earth-creature can live. They dominated the...*water.* The Zeebs came. The Zeebs conquered. And there was nothing the humans could do.

Whoa! Sounds like sci-fi, right? Time to call in some action-adventure heroes? No. That's just the movies. The Zeebs are real. They really are aliens, and they really have invaded Ohio's waters.

But don't freak. One thing about Zeebs is that they hardly ever get any bigger than your thumbnail. And they didn't come here from another planet. An alien isn't only something from outer space. It can be any kind of creature or plant that is foreign, that comes from someplace else. It can even describe persons who are living in a nation where they are not citizens. Being alien really means that, whatever you are, you're not from around here.

"Zeeb" is my nickname for zebra mussels. And I don't mean little black-and-white striped horse-like critters that are into body-building. Zebra mussels are basically clams with sticky threads. They have dark brown shells with tan and white stripes. They have always lived in the freshwater seas of Russia. They slowly spread into the lakes, rivers and canals of Europe over the last couple hundred years.

Zeebs can't live in salty ocean water, so they couldn't cross the Atlantic by themselves. Instead, they hitched a ride on ocean-going ships. In 1959 Canada's St. Lawrence River was made deep enough to let huge ocean-going ships steam on through to the Great Lakes. It was only a matter of time before the mussels came along for the ride.

No one knows exactly what ship brought the first Zeebs nor exactly when. But in the 1980s scientists began to notice them on the rocks and shoreline algae of Lake Erie. You might say that the mussels meant no harm for they were just doing their thing. Each little Zeeb sucked in water, filtered out tiny bits of food and then spit the water out again. Even the biggest zebra mussel can filter only a quart of water in a day.

The trouble is, they don't just filter-feed. They multiply. Each female can produce more than 300,000 eggs a year. Lake Erie turned out to be the perfect breeding ground for them, a Zeeb heaven. No one knows exactly why. Ohio's Great Lake is the shallowest and warmest of the five. Maybe that's the reason. By the mid-1990s there were millions and millions of zebra mussels. They blanketed rocks, docks, buoys, boats and any unfortunate plant or animal that would sit still long enough for Zeeb attachment.

The mussels were not only crowding the lake, they were cleaning it out. That might sound like a good thing, but it's not. They did such a good job filtering the food out of the water that they starved off the native Ohio mussels that were already living there. And they had been there for a very long time. When dinosaurs sloshed through ancient creeks, they crushed freshwater mussels underfoot. So what, you might ask.

Well, North America has more than 300 native kinds of mussels, more than anywhere else in the world. The species that live in Ohio are a link in the food chain, which means that other animals like to eat them. Without our native mussels lots of other wildlife would be affected. Some scientists are trying to move the native mussels into protected storage ponds at The Wilds (see Chapter 13, The Wilds). From there they could be re-stocked to Ohio rivers and ponds.

But it gets worse. As Lake Erie became cleaner and clearer, sunlight began to penetrate deeper into the waters. Some fish like murky waters because they need dark places to lay their eggs.

Worst of all, the Zeebs hitched rides on boat trailers from Lake Erie to other Ohio lakes and rivers. The mussels again searched for hard surfaces to settle on. They soon were crowding in thick and heavy on the pipes that bring water into treatment plants, factories and our houses. Almost a million can squeeze into a single square yard. They can plug things up so tight that the water can't flow through.

Once the problems began, the Zeebs made the news. Some newspaper headlines claimed that the zebra mussel invasion was worse than an oil spill. Others predicted that in a few years the mollusks would turn the Ohio River bright green. A few people got a bit carried away and even claimed that the Russians, our enemies during the long Cold War, had sent the tiny animals on purpose to destroy our waters and "The American Way of Life."

What to do? Well, water companies tried to kill Zeebs with

heavy doses of chlorine. It didn't work very well and it made the water taste funny. In desperation someone tried a powder made from berries that grow on the mountain slopes of Ethiopia. The powder is supposed to poison Zeebs without hurting other life forms. But the berries have to be handpicked, which is a lot of expense and bother. And then someone really got carried away and suggested draining Lake Erie and letting it sit dry for a couple of years. That would do away with the Zeebs, for sure, at least for a while.

But then, Mother Nature may take care of the problem on her own. Some biologists are seeing freshwater sponges that have been springing up all of a sudden. Perhaps they will smother the Zeebs?

In truth, the zebra mussels may not be all bad. True, they've knocked out a lot of native species and that's not good for the food chain. But if some kinds of fish seem fewer in the cleaner, clearer water, others are more plentiful. Some water plants are coming back in Lake Erie that have not been seen since pioneer days. And the zebra mussel population seems to be stabilizing, all on its own. When alien species invade, they can take over for a while. But then, gradually, they often find their place in the scheme of things.

A biologist with the Ohio Department of Natural Resources summed it up this way: "We're not happy with them, but zebra mussels really haven't done a lot of harm. And, anyway, life goes on." That seems to be the bottom line: Life goes on, Zeebs or not.

To learn more...

Exotic Invaders by Jeanne M. Lesinski (Walker and Company, 1996) includes impressive photographs

Toad Overload by Patricia Seibert (The Millbrook Press, 1996) tells another tale of a different alien species run amok

Mussels, Hard-Shelled Mollusks by Andreu Llamas (Secrets of the Animal World series, Gareth Stevens, 1997) provides a thorough introduction to mussel biology

Web sites

http://sun.science.wayne.edu/~jram/zmussel.htm (great slide show and links)

http://seagrant.wisc.edu/greatlakes/glnetwork/exotics.html (other alien species)

www.ag.ohio-state.edu/~earthsys/zebra.html (OSU's interactive zebra mussel quiz)

16

Ohio's Elephants

Did you know that Ohio has a permanent population of elephants? As I drive around the state, I sometimes see them out of the corner of my eye, marching down the side roads. (Just kidding, just kidding!) Now, read on for the truth.

Remember that woolly mammoth back in Chapter 2? Remember what he did to those Ohioans who came after him with spears? He stomped the stuffing out of them! Well, things have changed. Elephants don't roam freely in Ohio anymore. And Ohioans don't hunt them. But elephants do live here. Ohio has a permanent population of about 15 pachyderms. (That's a funny-sounding word for thick-skinned, non-ruminant ungulates. What? I mean *elephants*!) Don't worry. You won't stumble onto a herd of them out in the country somewhere. Not yet anyway (see Chapter 13, The Wilds). Ohio's elephants all live in zoos located in Toledo, Cleveland, Columbus and Cincinnati.

As of 2002, the youngest Ohio elephant lives in Cincinnati. And he is the most famous one, too, by far. Why? Because at 4:50 a.m. on March 15, 1998, he became the first elephant to be conceived and born in Ohio since the days of the woolly mammoths. That spring day marked the first time in more than 10,000 years that a newborn baby elephant blinked at Ohio sunlight and sniffed Ohio air.

It was a very big deal. Thousands crowded into the zoo to catch a glimpse of him. As soon as he was ready to meet the public, our family went and waited in a long line just to see this newborn baby. He was three feet tall and awfully cute, with his long eye-lashes, kindly gaze and all that fuzzy hair. He could walk almost right away but he was careful to stay very close to his mom.

This newborn elephant made news all over the world. It's very difficult for zoo elephants to have babies. No one knows just why. For some reason, it's much easier for elephants to have babies when they live in herds, in the wild. So when this 213-pound zoo baby came along, he made a big splash.

The zoo had a contest asking people to name the newborn. There were thousands of entries. Finally, the baby elephant's name was announced. He would be called Ganesh.

So why'd the zoo choose that name? Ganesh is a much beloved god in the Hindu religion, practiced by almost 800 million people throughout the world, especially in India. The story of Ganesh is long and involved, and somewhere along the way, the god found that his normal human head had been replaced by the head of an elephant. The great elephant-headed Ganesh is the god of knowledge and is very wise. He is called upon at the beginning of anything important—starting a trip, arranging a wedding or taking a test in school. If you follow the Hindu faith and you want your dreams to come true, you must have Ganesh on your side. Hindus are very fond of Ganesh and his long curving trunk, tusky smile, pot-belly and big flappy ears. Since this Cincinnati newborn was an Indian elephant and he represented the beginning of something very important, the name fit.

Oddly enough, Ohioans can see a statue of this Hindu god over the main entrance to the farmhouse at Malabar Farm State Park (see Chapter 11, Louis Bromfield's Amazing Pig). The owner of the farm wasn't Hindu, but he must have wanted Ganesh on his side.

Ganesh, the baby elephant, has gotten on very well since we first saw him. Every time we visit the zoo, we're amazed to see how much he's grown. And he will probably live to enjoy another 50 or 60 years.

In the zoo, he will be safe. In the wild, lions and hyenas often kill and eat baby elephants. But baby elephants' fiercest enemies are the poachers who shoot their mothers for their meat and for their ivory tusks. And in some countries humans have destroyed or taken over the elephants' territory and left them with little to eat and even less to feed their babies.

All his life Ganesh will have plenty to eat. From day one he sucked gallons of perfectly formulated milk straight from his mother. When he's full grown he may eat—every day!—300 pounds of new plant shoots, green leaves, fruit, grass, tree branches and soft bark. And he may drink 50 gallons of water a day. (How many full bathtubs is that?) He may grow to be 10 feet tall and may weigh as much as three tons.

Everything about Ganesh is amazing, even the bottoms of his feet. They're covered with thick pads so that, if he wants to, he can tiptoe very quietly. And I'm told that on hot summer days Ganesh sweats only one place—around his toenails! Honest!

Don't worry about his getting too hot, though. His leathery ears will help keep him cool. And they'll help him tune into many sounds that are too low for human ears to hear. He will use his ears more than his eyes to learn about his world.

But the number-one thing he will use for exploring is his amazing trunk. He'll use it for smelling, touching, picking up food and for sucking up water to hose into his mouth when he's thirsty. He'll use it to give himself a shower of water or a puff of dust. Right from the start, his trunk has been packed with thousands and thousands of small muscles. His trunk will grow to be a very useful power tool, helping him lift a whole tree if he wants to. Yet Ganesh will also be able to handle tiny things with his trunk, things as delicate as a blade of grass. He'll become so skillful that, with his trunk alone, he will be able to pick up a single peanut, crack it open, blow away the shell and eat just the kernels.

He'll use his trunk to greet other elephants. It's sweet to think that elephants say hello to one another with their noses. They touch each other's mouths with the tips of their trunks. And when some loud noise scares them a little, something like firecrackers on the 4th of July or a truck backfiring on a nearby street, an elephant will put its trunk into another elephant's mouth to let them know that they don't need to worry. It's their way of saying that everything is okay.

But for now Ganesh is still a little kid, and mainly he is busy playing. He wrestles, pretends to fight and plays tag. He likes to splash in the water just as human children do.

The other elephants care about Ganesh and they all help in raising him. They teach him what to eat and how to eat. They show him how to bathe and roll in the mud to protect his skin from the hot sun. He learns from them not to fear the zookeepers. The older elephants are always nearby, protecting Ganesh from danger, imparting elephant wisdom and letting him know that everything really is okay. Maybe they want Ganesh to grow up and, like his Hindu namesake, offer protection and blessings to the next generation of Ohio-born elephants.

To learn more…
Elephants by Karen Dudley (Raintree Steck-Waughn 1997)
Elephants by Annette Barkhausen and Franz Geiser (Gareth Stevens, 1994)
Elephant by Ian Redmond (Eyewitness Books, Alfred A. Knopf, 1993)

Little Orphan Elephants by Ellen Lambeth, in *Ranger Rick,* July 2001; vol. 35 (7), pp 4-9

In the Wild: Elephants by Claire Robinson (Heinemann, 1997)

The Elephant-Headed God and Other Hindu Tales by Debjani Chatterjee (Oxford University Press, 1992)

The Complete Just So Stories by Rudyard Kipling (Viking, 1993) includes the classic tale of how the elephant got its trunk in "The Elephant's Child"

Visit Ohio pachyderms at these locations:

The Columbus Zoo, telephone (614) 645-3550 or log on www.colszoo.org

The Cincinnati Zoo, telephone (513) 281-4700 or 1-800-94-HIPPO or log on www.cincyzoo.org

The Cleveland Metroparks Zoo, telephone (216) 661-6500 or log on www.clemetzoo.org

The Toledo Zoo, telephone (419) 385-5721 or log on www.toledozoo.org

Web sites:

www.pbs.org/wnet/nature/elephants (African elephants)

http://abcnews.go.com/sections/science/dailynews/elephant_india000605.html (Indian elephants and related stories)

www.kamat.com/kalranga/festive/ganesh/4867.htm (information about Ganesh)

17

Ohio Bird Sanctuary

I admire people who help animals, especially injured animals. The animals will never say "Thank you!" to these people. They can't, of course. But I can. This story is my way of thanking all those good people.

A whistle pierces the air. Phoenix, high above, cocks his head and spies a little girl far below. Suddenly he tips the edge of his wings, and drops—zooming straight down upon her at lightning speed. He is thinking of food! His powerful beak opens, his sharp talons stretch toward her!

Phoenix is magnificent. His head, back and chest are chocolate brown. He has reddish-gold shoulder patches and a broad white stripe on the end of his tail. His legs are a bright orange-yellow.

Phoenix is not the legendary bird that burns himself up and then rises anew from his own ashes. Phoenix is a Harris hawk. He lives at the Ohio Bird Sanctuary near Lexington, Ohio. His trainer, care-giver and best friend is nine-year-old Sarah Laux.

Sarah is happy to see Phoenix diving toward her when she whistles for him. There's a smile on her freckled face, for this is what she has trained Phoenix to do. Fearless, she tosses her shoulder-length brown hair. Her bangs flip to the sides of her striking blue eyes. She reaches toward the diving hawk. She wears a thick, heavy glove to protect her hand from his talons. On the glove Sarah has placed a tasty snack for Phoenix. Seconds later, Phoenix is perching on the glove, gobbling down his treat—a delicious dead mouse.

Sarah's mom is Gale Laux, the director of the sanctuary. It's a place where birds are loved and protected. The facility's swamps, forests and fields are all full of birds. Some of them come and go while others live there year round.

Some year-round residents are kept captive there but only because they have been injured and cannot fly away. People from all over Ohio bring injured birds to the sanctuary, and Gale and her helper Jan Ferrell give them first aid. Sometimes the birds have to be fed through tubes or given shots. These two women can do everything but surgery. (A local vet handles operations.)

Sometimes wounded birds have to be trained to fly or swim again. When a Muscovy duck with a broken leg was brought in, young Sarah knew just what to do. She wrapped the leg to the body until it could heal. She named the duck "Marble." For ten days Sarah fed him and carried him wherever he needed to go. Then Sarah removed the wrap. She gently opened his webbed foot and stretched his leg. She did this every day, encouraging Marble. Finally he was able to swim again.

Sarah and her sister Samantha have raised ducks, hawks, owls, Canada geese and many other kinds of birds. When the birds need care at night, their mother sometimes brings them home with her. Their farmhouse has had loons in the bathtub and great blue herons in the laundry room.

Many times Sarah and Samantha have heard their mom tell bird stories, like this one:

"One November some people called to say that a red-tailed hawk was coming up to their house and begging for food. He didn't move right and they knew he was injured. They threw him bits of hot dog and finally caught him with a net. When they brought him in, we found that his foot had been caught in a leghold trap. That was why he couldn't hunt for food on his own. The vet had to remove one of his toes, but it healed up fine.

"But even after two months the bird still couldn't fly right. Finally we figured out why. Looking beneath the feathers on his breast, we found that he had once been shot through the chest. The bullet had passed right on through. Somehow it hadn't killed him. But he had a hole in his chest muscle and it was full of old feathers. Back to the vet we went. The plug of feathers was removed and he began to heal once again. We kept him with us all through that winter.

"Finally, in April, he was all better. We took him back to the place where he had been found and let him loose. As he rose into the air, he was instantly joined by a beautiful female. She was his mate! All through the long winter she had been waiting there for him to return. She didn't know where he was or what was happening to him, but she never gave up hope. After all he'd been through, to hook up with his girlfriend again like that! And right away, too! What a happy ending!"

Gale's helper Jan Ferrell can hoot just like Apollo, a barred owl that lives permanently at the sanctuary. It's a weird hoo-whooo-hoo-hoo sound, but Jan has it down pat. She explains their name: "They're called barred owls for the dark brown bars that run up and down the tummy. Apollo looks like a great big toasted marshmallow!"

She tells how Apollo fell out of a tree when he was a few weeks old. Some people rescued him, but they didn't know how to care for him. Soon he was nearly starved to death. They brought him to the sanctuary and Jan took over. "Now he's healthy and all grown up but he thinks he's a human," Jan says. "He thinks he looks just like us and because of that we can't release him back into the wild."

Every day for five years Jan hooted at Apollo. He just looked at her with his great solemn eyes. Then one day he began to answer. Now whenever Jan comes to work, Apollo hoo-whooo-hoo-hoos at her first. She laughs. "It's like he's inviting me to come visit him in his nest!" she says.

Jan has a son Evan who's the same age as Sarah. Like Sarah,

he handles birds lots of kids don't even know about. Most Saturday nights he goes with his mom to Mohican State Park. On the way, Evan keeps his eyes open. While some kids might say they see just a bird, any old bird, Evan can recognize dozens of bird species at a glance. He doesn't see "birds"—he sees a red-tailed hawk, a kestrel or a peregrine falcon.

Jan puts on a bird show for guests at the park lodge. As soon as she gets out of the car, the show starts. Jan sends a hoo-whooo-hoo-hoo into the night. Often five or six owls come fluttering to her out of the dark. Evan knows just how his mom makes that hooting sound, but he can't hoot. Not yet. His voice is still too high. In a few years, when his voice changes, he'll be able to hoo-whooo-hoo-hoo just like Jan, just like a barred owl.

"When I grow up, I want to be a naturalist like my mom," Evan says. He wants to work at the Ohio Bird Sanctuary. Knowing how to hoot will sure come in handy.

To learn more...
Raptors: The Eagles, Hawks, Falcons, and Owls of North America by Ann Price and Roger Peters (Court Wayne, 2001)
The Peregrine Falcon: Endangered No More by Mac Priebe (Mindfull Publishing, 2000)
Eyewitness: Eagles & Birds of Prey by Jemima Parry-Jones (DK Publishing, 2000)

Sources that feature the call of the barred owl:
All About Owls by Jim Arnosky (Scholastic Inc., 1995)
The Book of North American Owls by Helen Roney Sattler (Clarion Books, 1995)
www.raptor.cvm.umn.edu (Raptor Center spotlights hawks, owls and eagles)
www.neoperceptions.com/fauna/birds/scbirds/bardowl.htm (calls with photographs)

Web sites
www.ohiobirdsanctuary.org (Ohio Bird Sanctuary or call 419-884-HAWK)
www.ohioparks.net/mohican (Mohican State Park)
www.Audubon.org (National Audubon Society includes a special kids' page)

18

Toad Tuning at Cedar Bog

When you first think about it (if you think about such things at all), the toad may not seem to be an especially amazing animal. But I'm sure you'll change your mind after reading about its surprising musical abilities.

When someone told me that toads sing, I thought they were pulling my leg. But it's true. The male toads sing, anyway. Or trill, more like. At least, that's what I heard Terry Jaworski say when I visited Cedar Bog.

Terry is a great big beefy bear of a man. "In my whole life," he says, "nobody ever called me Shorty." He has a heavy brown mustache and a heart of gold that shines through when he talks to kids. He's a born teacher. When he gives tours of Cedar Bog, he waves his arms, rolls his eyes and makes funny faces. He has a lot of funny little sayings to help you learn. Maybe that's just the way he speaks. Or maybe, after giving thousands of tours of Cedar Bog, he's found tricks that make people like to listen. He has a lot to say. He's been the naturalist at Cedar Bog since the mid-1970s. He knows the place inside and out. Plants, animals, soil—you name it. "I've got 18,000 years of Ohio's environmental history, right in here!" he says, swooping his thick arms around his head.

Cedar Bog is a famous nature preserve in Champaign County, Ohio, a few miles south of Urbana on Rt. 68. Mr. J., as Terry likes to be called, tells how the highway was once a buffalo run and later a Shawnee trail. Hearing him talk, you can imagine the thundering herds as if it were just last week, and the Shawnees just yesterday. Mr. J. makes the long ago seem very near.

But long ago at Cedar Bog really means the Ice Age, when mammoths drank from melting glaciers. "At the end of the Ice Age, Ohio was in a continuous spring," Mr. J. explains. "It never got colder than 22° and never warmer than 60°." In these spring-like temperatures the Ice Age plants died, except in the icy, limey water of the bog.

You see, the water at Cedar Bog doesn't come trickling in from surrounding hillsides, warmed by the sun. Instead Cedar Bog water comes bubbling straight up through limestone gravel from cold springs deep in the ground. (This type of bog is really called a fen, but that's another story.) The water stays pretty much the same temperature all year. It doesn't freeze, but it never gets warm. It's like a little lost world, an island of numbing coldness left over from the Ice Age.

That's why many plants in the bog are not commonly seen in Ohio. Northern white cedar—a type of pine—grows in the bog. So does dwarf birch. Nowadays these trees are normally found hundreds of miles to the north, up in the Canadian cold. They have a very short summer up there, so the plants are used to growing for just a few months every year. So they grow very, very slowly. They stretch out their lives and can survive as long as a thousand years. There are plenty of trees in Cedar Bog right now that were saplings on the day Columbus landed in 1492.

Wait a minute! What's Christopher Columbus got to do with toads singing opera? Well, I never said "opera," but sure, we'll get to the toads.

But first, you've just *got* to hear about sedges! Cedar Bog has sedges—plants that look like grass but have triangle-shaped stems. (Use scissors to cut across a hollow grass stem, and you'll get tiny circles. Cut across a sedge stem and you'll get a handful of perfect triangles.) "Sedges have edges," Mr. J. reminds you, waving at a meadow of sedges. When the 11,000-year-old remains of a mastodon (cousin of the mammoth) were discovered in Licking County, scientists dug around inside its stomach and found its last meal. Mr. J. read about it. "They found 18 different sedges, buds from a northern black willow and hackberry seeds—all plants that still grow here at Cedar Bog." Mr. J. invited the head scientist to come and see the Ice Age sedge meadow for himself. Mr. J. showed him, "There's your mastodon's last meal!"

Sedge roots lock together, making a spongy floor in the slippery gray soil of the swamp. (The limestone dissolved in the water makes the dirt turn gray.) But you still need to watch out for quicksand. Mr. J. has sunk right up to his chest, several times. He had trouble getting out. "Lost my shoes and almost my pants!" he laughs.

Wait a minute!! What's quicksand go to do with singing toads? We're getting there.

But first, let's take a quick tour with Mr. J.—we'll learn something with every step. Spice bush smells spicy, but don't expect the cinnamon fern to smell like cinnamon—it's named for its brown color. Thorn bugs make loving parents—most insects could care less. Musclewood and basswood are trees that live in water—with "wet feet" as Mr. J. puts it. The sundew is a plant that tempts you with droplets of honey-like sap. (If you happen to be a fly, beware. With its sticky sap it traps, kills and sucks the innards out of insects. If you think that's gross, Mr. J. will point out, "You eat plant sap, too. Maple syrup!")

Many rare species also find sanctuary in the wetlands and its clear icy waters. You might see fish, birds and butterflies you've never seen before. Or you might get lucky and meet the massasauga, a rare swamp rattlesnake. Another rare reptile is Kirtland's water snake. Mr. J. has sighted this snake only twice. But he knew it right away by its bright red belly.

But what about those singing toads? Okay, okay, let Mr. J. tell it. "On the first spring night when the temperature hits 60°, male toads come back to the pond where they were born. This is strange because toads live all year on the land, not in the water. But they do come back and begin trilling as loud as they can, to signal the females. A hundred of them singing at once can be *really* loud! So loud that people have to go 20 feet away to hear each other talk. Sometimes it starts about 4 a.m. My house is just a little way from the pond and when they start, it sounds like I have toads on the pillow right next to me!

"When the lady toads hear that trilling, they head for the pond. They're carrying 5,000 eggs and are twice as big as the males. Each lady toad tries to get next to the loudest singer. When she finds him, the male climbs on her back and hooks his thumbs under her armpits. Neither one can get loose. For the next 24 hours the lady drags her rider through the sticks and the muck. All during this wild ride she pushes out eggs in a long string, and he pushes out fluid. The eggs and fluid meet and then slowly grow into toadpoles. Toadpoles? Hey, if baby frogs are called *tad*-poles, I figure baby toads have just *got* to be called *toad*-poles!"

Crowds of people come to Cedar Bog every March to hear the toads sing. It's called a toad tuning. Some years ago another Ohio nature preserve claimed that their toads were bigger and more tuneful. There was a contest. Judges visited both preserves and Cedar Bog won. What was the prize?

"The Golden Toadstool A-wart," Mr. J. crows. "Not *award*. That's *a-wart*!"

To learn more...

Toads by Amanda Harman (Grolier Educational, 2001)

Frogs and Toads: The Leggy Leapers by Sara Swan Miller (Franklin Watts, 2000)

Amphibians by Dr. Barry Clarke (Eyewitness Books, Alfred A. Knopf, 1993)

Wetlands by Vicki Leon (Silver Burdett Press, 1999)

Mysteries of the Bog by Louise E. Levathes (National Geographic magazine, March 1987)

Sundews: A Sweet and Sticky Death by Victor Gentle (Gareth Stevens Publications, 1996)

Web sites

www.ohiohistory.org/places/cedarbog (arrange a visit, or call 800-860-0147)

www.dnr.state.oh.us/dnap/location/kentbog.html (view the Kent Bog aerial photograph)

www.dnr.state.oh.us/dnap/mapofpreserves.htm (Ohio Department of Natural Resources lets you click on a bog, fen or marsh close to your home)

www.ohiodnr.com/wildlife/resources/amphibians/amphibians_files/v3_document.htm (amphibians and links)

www.epa.gov/owow/wetlands/types/fen.html (fens and bogs)

www.carnivorousplants.org/gallery/gallerymain.html (photos of carnivorous plants)

www.yahooligans.com/Science_and_Nature/Living_Things/Replites_and_Amphibians/ (provides useful links)

www.brocku.ca/envi/jm/massasauga (click on Mr. J.'s report about the massasauga rattler)

www.dcnr.state.pa.us/wrcf/ksnake.htm (Kirtland's water snake)

19

Canada Geese

Once I was deep in the woods near Bellville when I heard a sound like hundreds of barking dogs, heading in my direction. The racket got louder, fast! So fast, it scared me! Then I looked up. It was a flock of Canada geese, honking their hearts out as they passed overhead.

One time when I was visiting a school, a student asked me, "If you could change into any animal, which one would you be?" Well, I didn't have to think about it. I knew right away what animal I'd be. "A Canada goose," I told him.

"A *goose*? You'd be a *goose!?*" He couldn't believe it.

"Not just a goose," I explained. "A *Canada* goose. You know, those great big beautiful brown and white birds that soar above the earth in a V-shaped formation?"

But he didn't know what I was talking about. He wasn't even listening. I heard him whispering to his classmates, his thumb pointing at me. "A goose! He'd be a goose!" He smacked his hand to his forehead and rolled his eyes.

Maybe he was thinking of those big, white barnyard geese. That wasn't what I meant. Or maybe he was imagining me as Mother Goose, wearing a bonnet and a cape. That *certainly* wasn't what I meant.

I was sorry to disappoint him. Maybe I could have named many other animals that would have seemed much cooler to him. A cheetah. A shark. An eagle. A python. A T-rex. And what did I come up with? A goose. Dumb old author.

But I meant it. Don't get me wrong. I enjoy being a human, all told. I wouldn't want to change for keeps. But if I could become any animal for an hour and then change back to being human again, I really would choose to be a Canada goose.

I'd like to join my geese friends as part of a flying wedge. Think of it! To be able to fly high in the sky, fearless, and on strong wings. To look far, far ahead or down on passing fields, forests and lakes. And to soar with others who share my values, who feel the same way I do about things. (The only time I get that feeling—as a human—is when I'm singing in my church choir.) But Canada geese must have that joy every time they take to wing.

The famous V formation helps to keep the geese from tiring too much as they fly. The goose at the point of the V punches a hole in the air with each downbeat of his wings. As he moves forward, he breaks a wedge into the air. The other geese in the chevron make the wedge wider and wider until the whole formation passes through. The point goose does get tired, though. It's hard work punching through air! So, every half hour or so, the geese trade positions in the V. Each one takes a turn at the point. I think that would be fun.

And to be such a beautiful creature! I mean, I'm handsome enough, I suppose, for a middle-aged human male. But a Canada goose is gorgeous, with that noble jet-black neck and head and dashing white patch on the cheek! Its bill, legs and feet are black as night. The feathers that cover its strong body are in fashion— from slate gray to dark-chocolate brown.

I agree with their family values. Canada geese choose one mate and then stick with them their whole life. That fits my style. I've been married to the same nice lady for 30 years. The two geese take care of their young together. My wife and I reared our son and daughter together.

I admire their courage. Canada geese aren't wimps. They're feisty! They have enemies, but they stand up to them. All kinds of creatures try to sneak up and eat the eggs or newborn hatchlings, from crows to coyotes, from hawks to groundhogs.

Geese guarding their eggs or hatchlings are fearless. If another animal or a human comes too near, watch out! They can get riled up enough to fling all their weight right at you, honking and hissing, clapping their bill, ruffling their feathers, flapping their big powerful wings. They don't bite or scratch. Geese don't have teeth or talons, but they can nip! When you turn to run, they chase after you, nipping your behind.

Be very careful if you meet an enraged Canada goose face to face and the bird attacks. It can whack really hard with its wings! But when encounters between humans and geese result in injuries, it's usually because the people get really scared, turn to run, and then fall over a stump or curb or slam into a tree or fence.

Another reason I love these magnificent birds is because they still seem fresh and exotic to me. Kids today are used to Canada geese. They see them often. Nowadays, Ohio is splashed with ponds surrounded by grass, set in parks, golf courses or corporate headquarters. Some of the ponds even have fountains that keep the water from freezing in winter. These are perfect places for Canada geese, especially flocks that have stopped migrating, or flying south for the winter. And if humans feed the geese (instead of blasting them with guns), the birds lose their fear of people. (See Chapter 24, Bud the Wonder Dog, for a story about a flock that hung around the wrong "perfect" place.)

When I was a boy, back in the 1950s, I never saw a Canada goose. It's hard to believe, I know. But they just weren't around. In fact, some subspecies of Canada geese were thought to be extinct. They were here in the pioneer days but were nearly wiped out by hunters. The swamps that had been their homes were drained to make farmland.

Then Ohio changed its hunting laws and created some wetlands wildlife refuges. Some small flocks, safe in pens at the state wildlife sanctuaries, began to breed. The goslings (geese old enough to be on their own) were allowed to fly away. Geese always return to the area where they learned to fly, so the numbers in the wildlife areas slowly grew. By the 1980s geese spilled out of wildlife areas and into the rest of the state. When I first started seeing them, in my thirties, I could hardly believe my eyes. I had no idea such a majestic bird was living in my state!

Today there are more than two million Canada geese. They've become common, but I still feel a thrill every time I see them.

So, now you know why I'd like to be a Canada goose. I don't think my young friend ever quite got over the shock of it. The last time I saw him, he was still slapping his temples with both hands and shaking his head back and forth.

"A goose!" he kept saying. "Rick Sowash wants to be a goose!"

To learn more...
City Geese by Ron Hirschi (Dodd, Mead & Company, 1987)
Honk, Honk by Mick Manning and Brita Granstrom (Kingfisher, 1997) fiction
The Way Home by Nan Parson Rossiter (Penguine Putnam Books, 1999) fiction

Sources for adult readers, but with stunning photographs:
Father Goose by William Lishman, photographs by Joseph Duff (Crown Publishers,
    1996) (available as a VHS video) takes you with the author on migration
The Canada Goose by Kit Howard Breen (Voyageur Press, 1990) follows the geese
    through the four seasons

Web sites

www.kidzone.ws/animals/birds/canada-goose.htm (more about Canada geese)

www.enchantedlearning.com/subjects/birds/printouts (color a goose—or robin, or moa!)

www.utm.edu/departments/ed/cece/trugeese2.shtml (subspecies of Canada geese)

20

Guide Dogs

*You've probably been touched, as I have been,
when you see blind people escorted by guide dogs.
Did you ever wonder how those dogs
begin their training?*

In a small space, a woman and a dog are asleep. One is a killer with a dark past and a caged, almost empty future. The other doesn't have much of a past at all, but a joyful, glorious, even heroic future. Both are dreaming. The dog's feet make little running motions. The woman mumbles something and turns on her side. Which one is the killer?

The clue that will give you the answer, if you think about it, is the phrase "in a small space." The small space is a prison cell. The woman is the killer. I don't know her story and I don't need to know it. For me, it's enough that she killed another human being, was captured, tried, found guilty and imprisoned. She will probably spend the rest of her almost empty life at the Ohio Reformatory for Women, near Marysville, Ohio.

She is a real person, but I'm not going to describe her here. I'm not even going to use her real name. I hate it when television, books and newspapers make criminals famous by showing us their faces and telling us their names. I believe convicted killers don't deserve to have the public know their names. So I'm just going to call this woman "J."

But what about the dog? Oh, I'll tell you all about him. He's a puppy and his name is Lambert. He's a golden retriever, which many say is the best dog there is. His long fur is soft, warm and smooth. It's dazzlingly beautiful—a rich, shiny copper-red with blond highlights. His nose is big and black and wet and cold. His ears and tail are long and floppy. He's still a pup, so his legs seem a little too long for his body and his feet seem a little too big for his legs.

When he is full grown, he'll be magnificent. Lambert is already pretty good at following orders, and he is always ready and eager to play. But his eyes have a gentle, soulful look that make him seem old and wise.

Why is Lambert sharing a prison cell with a killer? Lambert is spending a year behind bars so that J. can train him to become a guide dog for a blind master. J. was carefully chosen for this job. Only the best-behaved prisoners are selected. J. must housebreak Lambert and get him used to being around people. She must teach him to obey basic commands such as sit, stay and heel. She must groom Lambert and clean up after him. And she must keep a careful journal about Lambert's progress and habits.

J. loves Lambert. She loves having this responsibility. "It's like being a mother," she says. "It gives you something to look forward to each day. Lambert is my best friend."

Lambert loves it too. In years to come, when Lambert is a guide dog, he will stay close to his blind master night and day. He's getting used to this kind of relationship by being with J. round the clock. This early training will help him to pay attention to his guide-dog work later on. He won't be as easily distracted by noises or smells or crowds of strangers.

Lambert came to J. through Pilot Dogs Inc., a Columbus-based organization that has placed guide dogs, without charge to blind people, since 1950. They began pairing puppies with prisoners in 1992.

When puppies first come to the Ohio Reformatory for Women, they are still very young. Right from the start, they are never far from their trainer. This is probably why 80 percent of the prison-raised puppies later qualify as guide dogs. When such dogs are raised in foster homes, only about 60 percent qualify. Homes can be loving places, of course, but sometimes they can also be almost too busy. Inmates have little to do other than to train their dogs.

There are now more than 500 guide dogs that got their basic training from inmates. Golden retrievers are not the only breed in the program. German shepherds also make great guide dogs as do Labrador retrievers and poodles. (That's strange. I often think of poodles being walked on the sidewalks of Paris by fancy models or movie stars—not caged with a drably-dressed Ohio convict.)

Speaking of sidewalks, the one problem with training guide-dog puppies in prison is that the convicts can never give them any training outside the prison, on busy city streets. This is a serious problem. A dog that is afraid of honking horns and moving automobiles cannot be a good guide dog. But the Marysville prison found a solution. Members of a local Lions Club volunteer to walk the puppies in town every weekend. That does the trick.

When Lambert leaves the Ohio Reformatory for Women, he will be paired with a blind master. Pilot Dogs will use J.'s journal to choose the best human for his personality. Then he will train alongside his new master for another four months. Then at last, Lambert will be a fully trained guide dog and will begin his joyful, glorious, even heroic future.

J. doesn't like to think about the day when Lambert has to leave. She knows she will never see Lambert after that and is very sad about it. After Lambert moves on, she will probably be given another dog to train. But that doesn't lessen the feeling of loss. If you've ever lost a dog and then gotten a new dog, you know about this. "It's going to be like giving up a best friend," she says. "All the convicts in the program feel this way. But we'll know that somebody else who really needs them is going to get loving dogs who are loved by us."

J. is a convicted killer, but she still has the ability to love. And she still wants to offer something to the rest of the world. "Now that I'm in prison," she said, "just about the only way I can help anyone else is by raising my puppy well."

We'll be very quiet as we leave these two, sleeping and dreaming, side by side...in a small space.

To learn more…

Guide Dogs by Charles and Linda George (RiverFront Books, 1998)

Guide Dogs, Seeing for People Who Can't by Alice B. McGinty (PowerKids Press, 1999)

A Guide Dog Puppy Grows Up by Caroline Arnold (Harcourt, Brace Jovanovich, 1991)

Buddy, the First Seeing Eye Dog by Eva Moore (Hello Reader! Series, Scholastic, 1996)

Teacher's Pet by Laurie Halse Anderson (Pleasant Company Publications, 2001)

Web sites

www.canismajor.com/dog/pilot.html (raising Pilot Dog puppies in homes)

http://enquirer.com/editions/1998/05/27/4313.html (Pilot Dogs in prisons)

www.puppiesbehindbars.com/main/html (a New York prison program)

www.circletail.org (Circle Tail Inc. provides assistance dogs for various disabilities)

www.seeingeye.org (The Seeing Eye, the original American guide dog institute)

www.guidedogs.com (Guide Dogs for the Blind, Inc.)

www.guidedog.org (Guide Dog Foundation for the Blind, Inc.)

www.guiding-eyes.org (Guiding Eyes for the Blind)

www.acb.org/index.html (The American Council for the Blind assists the visually impaired)

21

Guide Horses

*Some say that the glory days for horses ended
when the automobile came along. Not so.
Consider the story of Roger Bemiller and Blaine.*

Roger Bemiller's best friend is a horse named Blaine and he's almost invisible. Almost invisible to Roger, that is. You see, Roger is nearly blind. He was born with a disease that slowly caused his eyes to fail. There is no cure. He can make out things, somewhat, if they're close up, but everything else just looks like shades of light and dark to him. He is completely blind in bright sunlight. He can't see his farmhouse or the barns out back.

As the years passed, his worsening sight destroyed his confidence. He drove a car for the last time in 1984. He could no longer read street signs and was declared legally blind. Then he was divorced. Living alone on a little farm in rural Knox County, Ohio, Roger grew deeply sad. Nothing interested him. For years he sat alone with his television, listening to re-runs he couldn't see. He left his farm only when someone drove him to and from a grocery in nearby Fredericktown. Just a handful of friends stayed with him through all those troubles.

Then one of those loyal friends had an idea. He suggested that Roger learn to ride a horse again. It was something he hadn't done in 20 years.

Roger contacted Karen Sanchez, a riding instructor in Centerburg, Ohio. Karen operates Equine Assisted Therapy, a non-profit clinic for disabled people, mostly children. She taught Roger to ride again. Then she gave him a light-brown American quarter horse named Blaine. "He matches Roger's personality to a T", Sanchez says. "It's like they're best buddies."

Karen also trained the 13-year-old horse to walk along roads and avoid cars and trucks. To get to the grocery in Fredericktown, Roger and the horse must cross State Route 13, a dangerous, heavily used highway. But the horse knows to stop and wait for traffic to clear. "I trust him with my life every day," Roger says.

Usually we think of guide dogs helping the blind, not guide horses. In most situations a guide horse would be out of place. Just imagine trying to get on an elevator or into a restaurant with a horse! But what if you could make the horse the same convenient size as a guide dog? Now imagine a *tiny* horse leading you into an elevator or settling down under a restaurant table!

Roger needed a full-sized guide horse because he lived in a farm area and used Blaine as his wheels (so to speak), as well as his eyes. But most people who need guide animals live and work in towns and cities. They need a compact model, not much higher than their knees. And that's where miniature horses come into the picture. Miniature horses are about the size of a large German shepherd. They usually weigh between 55 and 100 pounds and certainly fit under restaurant tables.

Like guide dogs, miniature guide horses are intelligent, have great memories, and can be trained to ride in cars, elevators and escalators (as long as their tails are kept short enough so they don't get tangled in the moving steps). Both dogs and horses are natural guide animals. In the old days cavalry horses sometimes guided wounded soldiers back to safety. And both animals can be housebroken. When a miniature horse "needs to go," it is trained to make nickering noises or to paw at the door. A horse that has to go *really* bad will stomp its feet and cross its back legs. Both dogs and horses like to be groomed, brushed, petted and scratched. Miniature guide horses who live in houses like to lie on couches and beds. They can even be trained to sleep beside their owners. Rub a horse's tummy and it soon falls asleep.

But guide horses have some advantages over guide dogs. They don't get fleas, they have almost no odor and they don't have to be broken of the habit of stopping and sniffing everything! They may be perfect for someone allergic to dogs. Their eyes are on the sides of their heads, and this allows them to see in almost all directions at once. And they normally live to be about 30 years old, more than twice as long as most dogs. Instead of having to learn to work with three or four dogs over a lifetime, a blind person with a guide horse might be able to stay with just one animal.

Horses eat grass and so they make excellent lawn mowers. In the winter, when there is no fresh grass, they need a bale of hay each week plus a daily cup of oats. All horses love apples and candy, but owners must be careful not to overfeed them—and not just because too many sweets can make a horse fat and unhealthy. A guide horse with a taste for candy can make for other problems. On her first trip inside a grocery store, one guide horse snapped up a Snickers bar!

Owners must be careful, however, because horse hooves can be slippery. Rubber horse shoes, glued onto their hooves, can help horses stay steady on tile, waxed or hardwood floors. Outdoors, the horses can wear special horse-sneakers to protect their feet from hot pavements and broken glass.

Roger Bemiller's horse has done much more for him than simply getting him to the grocery and back. When he found that he really could get around on horseback, his confidence returned and he became a friendly person once more. Instead of just sitting home listening to old television shows, Roger now makes an almost daily round through Knox County. He chats with neighbors and keeps up with their doings.

A guide dog would have kept Roger too close to his own home. "If I had a dog, I'd have to walk everywhere," he says. "I can go farther distances with a horse. And Blaine has been sort of a door to meeting other people. When they hear his hoofsteps in the road outside their homes, people come out to be with me." Roger says that Blaine is the best thing that's ever happened to him.

Happy ending!!

To learn more...

Miniature Horses by Victor Gentle and Janet Perry (Garth Stevens, 2001)

Miniature Horses by Lynn M. Stone (Rouke Publishing, 2002)

Web sites

www.equineassistedtherapy.org (Equine Assisted Therapy helps the disabled gain confidence)

www.guidehorse.org (Guide Horse Foundation, with photographs of horse sneakers)

www.narha.org (North American Riding for the Handicapped Association)

www.amha.com (American Miniature Horse Association)

www.cavalry.org/immortal_horses.htm (stories of heroic horses)

22

Search and Rescue Dogs

*Disasters make news. As one reporter put it,
"We cover crashes, not landings." Yet most people
are safe, most of the time. Still, if you ever did need
rescuing, it's good to know that there are
animals like these dogs.*

You may not realize it but, right now, while you're quietly reading this page, there's a dog not far away who is ready, willing, able and eager to rescue you.

"Me?" you're thinking. "I don't need rescuing. I'm reading a book. I'm safe."

Hopefully, that's true. But what if there was, say, an earthquake?

An earthquake? In Ohio? Things like that don't happen here, you say. They happen in far off places like India or California. No, earthquakes don't happen in Ohio.

Wrong! In the years between the pioneer days and the present, Ohio had no fewer than forty dramatic earthquakes. In fact, one of the worst earthquakes of all time happened right here in the middle of America. Actually, it was a series of earthquakes. Seismologists still talk about it. (Seismologists study earthquakes.) They say it happened on the New Madrid fault, named for the river town in Missouri that was at the center of it all. (A fault is like a humongous crack in the earth where everything rips open in an earthquake.)

Missouri? That's a long way from Ohio. Nothing to worry about.

Wrong again! When the first quake hit Missouri in the wee hours of the morning of December 16, 1811, it sent a huge shock wave speeding toward Ohio at nearly 14,000 miles per hour. This was the first of four major quakes, and hundreds of smaller ones, that fanned out from Missouri like ripples in a pond, during the next two months.

Near New Madrid the ground shook so hard that no one could stand up. Trees split. The ground cracked open 10 feet wide in some places. Sand and water spouted as high as treetops. The riverbanks of the Mississippi caved in, making giant waves. Whole islands in the river disappeared while new ones sprang up from the muddy bottom. The thundering sound of the quake nearly split people's ears. And that was just the first quake. Two more great quakes followed some weeks later.

The worst and final quake hit on February 7, 1812 and lasted twenty-five minutes. In Ohio people in Chillicothe, Coshocton and Cincinnati saw tables and chairs jump across the floor. Doors banged open and then couldn't shut when the door frames bent. One man said that the shaking was so strong that it half emptied a bucketful of water sitting on the floor. In frozen rivers the ice cracked apart. Chimneys toppled over and wide cracks opened in the brick walls of buildings and houses.

The quakes were caused by two gigantic underground sections of rock splitting and grinding past one another at the New Madrid fault. This started 800 million years ago, right under the middle of our continent, and it's still there, grinding away. This means that the great New Madrid earthquakes will happen again. When? No one knows. They could begin at any moment—this afternoon, tomorrow, or not for 500 years or more.

In 1811 few people lived in Ohio. Cincinnati's population was just 2,500 then. Luckily, no one was hurt. But Ohio is very different today. When the earth quakes like that again, bad things will happen. Some homes and buildings will tumble down. Some people will be killed. And some people, still alive, will be trapped in the rubble.

Try to imagine it. One minute you're feeling safe, reading a book, maybe this one. Then, boom! Everything is shaking. Before you can even get up, the floor gives way, the walls cave in, the ceiling comes down and you're in the basement, trapped under a pile of boards, bricks and furniture. If you're still alive, maybe you're pretty badly injured. You probably can't dig yourself out. You're alone, in the dark, hurt and scared. It's hard to breathe. You yell, but no one can hear you. All you can do is wait.

That's when you need search and rescue (SAR) dogs to save you. These trained dogs are the quickest and surest way to find people buried in rubble. They do it by using their sense of smell, which is 40 times stronger in dogs than in humans. Even so, they must be trained and SAR training is long and intense. Their handlers train them by playing hide-and-go-seek at construction sites or junkyards. Someone hides in a pile of rubble. When the dogs seek them out, they get a doggy reward.

Only the best dogs can do it. They must be strong, smart and good at following orders. They must be able to stay calm in crowds of excited people. They must be able to ride in anything from helicopters to canoes or even in the buckets of bulldozers. And they must love to play hide-and-go-seek.

It's not just the dogs that need training. The handlers must learn too. They watch how their dogs act when finding people. Each SAR dog is different. Some wag their tails or just move their ears forward. Others whine, yip or bark.

The dogs work without leashes or dog tags so that they don't get tangled in the rubble. The dogs are very good at picking their way through broken glass and wreckage. To protect their paws, they wear special boots. The dog teams usually work four to six hours, resting between shifts. But they can work longer if needed, sometimes as long as 12 hours.

What do the dogs smell, exactly? Well, everywhere we go, each of us leaves behind a trail of hairs, breath, spit, sweat, oils and tiny skin flakes. All this together makes our individual smell, called our scent picture. It's like when a human sees a photo. So SAR dogs try to follow any human scent picture they can pick up.

Few police or fire departments have SAR dogs. Most often such dogs are owned and trained by volunteers. The Ohio K-9 Search Team, based in Columbus, is one such group. These people do their work for free purely for the love of helping others. And for the love of their noble SAR dogs.

Let's see now, where did we leave you? Hurt, scared, alone and buried in a dark pile of rubble. But what's this you hear? A dog is barking! You're found! Rescue workers come running with shovels and ropes. Soon, light breaks through. They lift you out and give you first aid. You're safe once more, thanks to the SAR dog.

To learn more...

Search and Rescue Dogs by Charles and Linda George (RiverFront Books, 1998)
Lighthouse Dog to the Rescue by Emily Harris (Down East Books, 2000)
Hugger to the Rescue by Dorothy Hinshaw Patent (Dutton Children's Books, 1994)
Animals Protecting Us by Robert Snedden (Watt, Franklin, 2000)
Earthquakes, Focus on Disasters by Fred Martin (Rigby Education Press, 1996)

For adult readers
The New Madrid Fault Finders Guide by Dr. Ray Knox and Dr. David Stewart (Gutenberg-Richter Publications, 1995) offers a thoroughly enjoyable field trip guide

Web sites

www.search-rescue.net/sarteamlinks.htm (links to all Midwest SAR teams)

www.nasar.org (National Association for Search and Rescue, Inc.)

http://hsv.com/genlintr/newmadrd (New Madrid earthquakes, photos and teaching aids)

http://newmadridonline.tripod.com (New Madrid, MO, through Civil War and earthquake)

www.ohiodnr.com/ohioseis (Ohio Seismic Network tracks earthquakes in Ohio and globally)

www.akc.org/love/cgc (American Kennel Club's Good Citizen Certificate for dogs)

23

A Hero Named LuLu

If you've read my book "Heroes of Ohio,"
you know my definition of heroes: they volunteer
to do something challenging that helps people.
By that definition, or by any other,
LuLu is a hero. There's no doubt about that!

Miracles have come to pass in my lifetime. One of the most amazing has been the comeback of Lake Erie. I can remember walking out onto the pier at Lakeside, Ohio in the 1950s with my parents. We didn't stay out there long. We couldn't stand it. The smell of sewage and dead fish was too strong. I can also remember my father's sadness when he told us how beautiful and fresh Lake Erie had been when he was a boy. Well, he lived long enough to see the rebirth of Lake Erie. The states that border the lake (and Canada) cleaned up their act, cracking down on the polluters. And today millions of people enjoy visiting Ohio's Great Lake once more.

They come to fish and boat and swim and picnic and set up tents and trailers. This is a fine thing. Still, where there are people, there are problems. And where there are problems, there are stories....

When Jo Ann Altsman arose on the morning of August 4, 1998, death was the furthest thing from her mind. She was vacationing at Lake Erie with her husband Jack and their two pets. After breakfast Jack went off fishing. Jo Ann was tidying up their vacation trailer when she suddenly felt a crushing pain in her chest. The pain quickly spread down her left arm and up into her jaw. She was sweating hard and couldn't get her breath. Her stomach was terribly upset and she was afraid she would faint.

Jo Ann was suffering a heart attack. Desperate for help, she pounded on the window until the glass broke. She cried out, "Help! Help! Call an ambulance!" But her cries were weak and no one heard them. She fell to the floor.

Both her pets were smart enough to know something was terribly wrong. The Altsman's American Eskimo dog began howling and barking. That did no good at all. But the Altsman's other pet knew just what to do and she did it.

The Altsman's other pet is LuLu, a solid-black Vietnamese pot-bellied pig. LuLu doesn't look much like a run-of-the-mill farmyard pig though she looks more like a pig than anything else. Vietnamese pot-bellied pigs are miniature size and weigh less than 200 pounds when full-grown. Typical full-grown American swine weigh 600 to 1,500 pounds. As adults, pot-bellied pigs grow to be about three feet long and 15 inches tall. LuLu was only one year old at the time of our tale, but she already weighed 150 pounds. She carried a lot of that weight in her sagging pot belly, which gives the breed its name.

Pot-bellied pigs, like pigs everywhere, are very smart (see Chapter 11, Louis Bromfield's Remarkable Pig). Like dogs, pigs can be trained to do tricks and to walk on a leash. They're *pigs*, after all, and they'll learn to do almost anything for food. They often figure out how to open their owner's fridge, cupboards, pantry—anywhere food might be found. But a *really* smart pig, like LuLu, can be a hero too.

LuLu looked at Jo Ann sadly. "She made sounds like she was crying," Jo Ann said later. Then LuLu pushed herself through the little piggy/doggy door Jack had cut into the side of the trailer. Jack had made the door wider and wider as LuLu grew, but it was a very tight fit on this day. Poor LuLu cut her pot-belly as she wriggled out the piggy/doggy door and into the fenced-in yard.

Her owners sometimes took LuLu for walks on a leash, but LuLu had never left the yard by herself. Nevertheless, she pushed long and hard on the gate, sprung the latch and boldly waddled to the edge of the road.

LuLu waited until she saw a car coming. Then she bravely made her way to the middle of the road and laid down, her pot-belly splaying out around her like a flounce dress. Cars swerved but didn't stop. Several times she went back to check on Jo Ann but then left again, determined to get help. One man stopped his car and stared at LuLu. Later he said he was afraid to get out because he didn't know what sort of creature she was. LuLu is very strange-looking. Even Jo Ann admits she's not very attractive.

Finally a driver stopped and got out of his car. When he drew near, LuLu jumped up and led him to the Altsman's trailer.

"I heard a man hollering through the door," Jo Ann reported afterward. When he told her that her pig was in trouble, Jo Ann called out, "*I'm* the one in trouble. Please get an ambulance!"

The man phoned 911 and help soon arrived. By that time, Jo Ann had been in terrible pain for 45 minutes. Fifteen more minutes, the doctors told her, and she might have been a goner. In the confusion and excitement, she never learned the kind man's name.

When the medics put Jo Ann on a gurney and rolled her into the back of the ambulance, LuLu tried to climb aboard. But the medics gently led LuLu back into the yard and fastened the gate tight, real tight. This pot-bellied pig had done enough for one day.

Jo Ann had an operation on her heart and is doing fine now. LuLu, the pot-bellied hero pig, became famous. At a fancy banquet in New York City, she was given a Trooper Award by the American Society for the Prevention of Cruelty to Animals.

Her fame and the award probably didn't mean all that much to LuLu. What she liked best was what Jack did when he came back from fishing. He knew just how to thank a pot-bellied pig. He didn't waste words—he gave LuLu a great big jelly doughnut!

To learn more...

Pot-Bellied Pigs: Weird Pets by Lynn M. Stone (Rouke Publishing, 2002)

Pigs by Sara Swan Miller (A True Book, Children's Press, 2000)

Pig Tales by Kate Tym (Element Children's Books Inc., 1999)

Ten True Animal Rescues by Jeanne Betancourt (A Little Apple Paperback, Scholastic Inc., 1998)

A Medal for Murphy by Melissa Forney (Pelican Publishing Company, 2000) fiction about another unattractive animal hero

Classic pig tales include *The Three Little Pigs* and *Charlotte's Web* (E.B. White*)*

Web sites

www.post-gazette.com/regionstate/19981010pig2.asp (LuLu's story and photograph)

www.petpigs.com (North American Potbellied Pig Association)

www.ncopp.com (National Committee on Pot Bellied Pigs)

http://netvet.wustl.edu/pigs.htm (links to everything porcine)

www.methodicalmagic.com/eskie/ (the all-white American Eskimo dog)

Just for fun

http://my.execpc.com/~scafativ/boris.html (Boris, a potbellied pig from Wisconsin)

www.geocities.com/cekatz (Dixie, another much loved potbellied pig)

www.muppets.com/piggy/piggy.htm (Miss Piggy, of course)

Bud the Wonder Dog

*Many wildlife species have come back to Ohio:
beavers, otters, eagles, wild turkeys and even bears.
Deer and Canada geese have done so well, in fact,
that they can become a problem.*

Mr. Niemie had a problem. This was okay with him. In fact it was his job, handling problems. Mr. Niemie is an elementary school principal. He solves all sorts of problems, all the time. Still, this one was tougher than most.

It was August. Mr. Niemie's summer vacation was over. He was happy and eager to get back to work. He had high hopes. It was going to be another great year at Bailey Elementary School in Dublin, Ohio.

When he pulled into the school parking lot, he was a little surprised to see a very large flock of Canada geese grazing on the school playground. "Such beautiful birds," he thought. "They must have stopped by on their way somewhere."

They seemed to like the schoolyard. The next morning they were still there. And the next morning. And the next. But it seemed they weren't hurting anything, so they were left alone to walk around, eating grass. Sometimes they would wander onto the blacktop part of the playground.

But one morning Mr. Niemie looked from his window and noticed that the blacktop where the geese wandered wasn't black anymore. It was green!

Mr. Niemie went out to take a closer look. The blacktop and most of the grass was thickly covered with stinky green slime. You can figure out what it was. No one would want to walk or run in grass like that. There could be no outdoor recess. The geese had to go, and soon. School started in three weeks.

Mr. Niemie knew he had to take action, slime or no slime. Necktie flapping, the principal charged headlong into the flock, yelling and waving his arms. The geese backed off as he came near, then crowded in again as soon as he passed. A few of them flew off a little ways but came back right away.

Later, as he bent over to clean his shoes with paper towels in the boys' restroom, Mr. Niemie was thinking. He needed more people to chase the geese. For several days Mr. Niemie had kids from a summer work program run about the playground, yelling and waving their arms. The only result was a bunch of tired kids with messy shoes.

Next, Mr. Niemie directed the school custodian to drive his truck right through the middle of the flock. This only made tire marks in the grass and didn't scare the geese one little bit.

Every morning Mr. Niemie counted the geese. There were more than 150. What to do? A crew came from the school district's central office to spray some evil-tasting stuff on the grass. It was supposed to make the geese leave. It didn't. Mr. Niemie talked to other principals, the school's treasurer, even the superintendent. No one knew what to do.

Problems with Canada geese are popping up everywhere. It's strange, because only 50 years ago, they were a rare sight (see Chapter 19, Canada Geese). They're not afraid of people (especially folks who are tossing bread, which really isn't good for them) and they've started to nest closer to buildings.

Then with just one week to go before the start of school, Mr. Niemie had an idea. He remembered a school assembly from the previous year when three of the Louwers family's border collies had done their tricks. (Danny, Nick, Andrew and Cathleen Louwers were all students at Bailey, and their grandfather trained these super-smart dogs.) The border collies had followed commands and herded a flock of ducks around the assembly hall.

When Mr. Niemie called the students' mom, Juli Louwers right away volunteered their family pet border collie Bud. She would bring him the next morning and give him a try.

Bud was a big old dog, 12 years old and 65 pounds big. He had floppy ears and long wavy hair. He was mostly black but had a pretty white tip on the end of his tail, white front legs, and a snowy cloak of fur around his neck, down his chest and under his belly. With brown on top of his eyes, like eyebrows, and touches of brown on his cheeks and hind legs, Bud was a good-looking dog.

The next morning Juli drove the family van to the school. She opened the door and Bud charged right out, making straight for the flock. Juli didn't have to give Bud any commands. He knew just what to do. After centuries of breeding and training, border collies know exactly how to herd animals. As he drew near the flock, Bud slowed his pace, got down low and began to creep up on the geese, staring at them, hard, all the while. Bud didn't bark. Border collies do their work in silence. Their power is in their stare. Bud would never hurt the geese, but they don't know that. The sight of a hard-staring dog creeping toward them is more than geese can stand.

The particular goose Bud stared at soon took off in a flurry of nervous flapping, followed by half the flock. Bud did the same thing to a few others and suddenly the playground was gooseless! Then Bud dashed back to Juli and Mr. Niemie. He sat right down next to them, proud of his work and waiting for the next job.

Well, Bud did his job for several days in a row. Finally, the geese got the idea that they weren't welcome at Bailey. They stayed away. Problem solved!

When the kids and teachers arrived and heard the story, they all wanted to meet the dog that had saved the school playground.

He became the hero of the school. They called him Bud the Wonder Dog and made him an official member of the school staff. They gave Bud an I.D. badge with his name and photo on it and even put his photo in the school yearbook, right along with the rest of the staff. At a special teachers' meeting Bud was given a steak and presented the "Friends of Educators Award."

Word has gotten around. These days Juli gets calls from schools, parks, golf courses and neighborhoods. They want Bud the Wonder Dog to rescue their grassy areas from Canada geese too.

In his old age Bud has found a glorious new career.

To learn more...
A Dog's Gotta Do What a Dog's Gotta Do: Dogs at Work by Marilyn Singer (Henry Holt Books for Young Readers, 2000)
Working Dogs by Sherry Shahan (Troll Communications, 2001)
Just Like Floss by Kim Lewis (Candlewick Press, 1998) fiction

For adults
The Versatile Border Collie by Janet E. Larson (Alpine Blue Ribbon Books, 1999)

Web sites
www.bordercollie.org (photographs and links to many border collie organizations)
http://schumer.senate.gov/SchumerWebsite/pressroom/press_releases/ PR01041.html (U.S. Senator Schumer discusses Canada geese problem)
www.american.edu/TED/GEESE.HTM (American University studies Canada geese problem)
http://suburban.gmnews.com/News/2001/0124/Front_Page/12.html (how Sayreville, NJ, handles the Canada geese problem)
www.theindependent.com/stories/091999/new_fowl19.html (Grand Island, NB, has a Canada geese problem)

Index

Aliens 86
American Indians
    Black Hoof 27
    Blue Jacket 27
    Little Turtle 26-29
    Moundbuilders 14-17
    Shawnee 20, 27
    Tecumseh 27
    tribes 27
Amish 65-71
Amphibians
Frogs 83, 107
Hellbenders 80-84
Salamanders 80-84
Toads 104-107
Audubon Society 41
Bald Eagle Act of 1940 60
"Big Muskie" 75
Birds
    Bald eagles 56-60
    Barred owls 100
    Canada geese 110-113, 140-143
    Hawks 99
    Muscovy Ducks 99
    Passenger pigeons 38-41
    Red-crowned cranes 74
    Robins 44-47
Bromfield, Louis 62-64
Cedar Bog 104-107
Celeste, Richard 5
Centerburg, OH 122
Champaign Co. 104
Chillicothe, OH 129
Cincinnati, OH 27, 31, 39, 41, 92, 93, 129
Cleveland, OH 39, 57, 92
Columbus, OH 4, 74, 92, 105, 117, 131
Coshocton, OH 129
Custer, George A. 29
Darke, William 29

Dayton, OH 3, 4, 45
Delaware Co. 38
Dogs
    American eskimo 134
    Border collie 141-143
    German shepherd 118, 123
    Golden retriever... 116, 118
    Guide dogs 116-119
    Labrador retriever... 118
    Pilot dogs 117
    Poodles 118
    Search-and-rescue 128-131
Dublin, OH 140
Earthquakes 128-129
Elephants 38, 77, 92-96
Fort Recovery, OH 28
Fossils 2-5
France 62, 74
Fredericktown, OH 122
Ganesh 93
Gatton (Cy, Earl, Nell) 50-52
Geneva, OH 58
Giraffes 74, 76
Great Serpent Mound 14-17
Halley's Comet 16
Hayes, Rutherford B. 34
Hemingway, Ernest 62
Herrick, Francis 57-60
Hindu religion 93, 96
Holmes Co. 68
Horses
    Guide horses 122-125
    Miniature 123-124
    Onager 74
    Przewalksi's 74
    Rienzi 32-35
Ice Age 8-11, 104-106
Kettering, OH 4
Knox Co. 122
Lake Erie 9, 57, 60, 87-89, 134
Lakeside, OH 134
Lexington, OH 98

Licking Co. 105
Lightning bugs 50-52
Malabar Farm 62-65, 93
Mammoths 8-11, 105
Marysville, OH 116
McConnelsville, OH 75
McKinley, William 34
Mercer Co. 26
Morgan, Arthur 3
Mounds 14-17
Muskingum Co. 74
Muskrats 68-71
Mussels 86-89
Ohio Bird Sanctuary 98
Ohio Reformatory for Women 116-118
Ohio River 14, 88
Opossums 20-23
Pigs 62-64, 135-137
Rabies 68-71
Richland Co. 49, 62, 64
Russia 87-88
St. Claire, Arthur 27-29
Sandusky Bay 59
Schorger, Arlie 38-41
Serpent Mound 14-17
Shaw, Fred 20-24
Sheridan, Philip 32-35
Shipman, Charles 56-60
Snakes 14-17, 106
Somerset, OH 32
Stein, Gertrude 62
The Wilds 74-77
Thorn bugs 106
Toads 104-107
Toledo, OH 92
Trilobites 2-5
Turtles 26
Urbana, OH 104
Vermilion, OH 57
Woolly mammoths 8-11
Zebra mussels 86-89
Zoos 41, 76, 93-95

The Author

Rick Sowash loves Ohio. He gathers up Ohio history, geography and folklore which he shapes into stories, books and musical compositions.

A veteran storyteller and a noted composer of classical music, Rick has logged thousands of performances around the world. He has also worked as a county commissioner, an arts administrator, a radio broadcaster, an innkeeper and a church musician.

He lives in Cincinnati with Jo, his wife of 31 years. They have two children, Shenandoah, 21, and John Chapman, 18.

Rick is also the author of a book of Ohio tall tales: "Ripsnorting Whoppers! Humor from America's Heartland" and a book of Ohio hero stories: "Heroes of Ohio: 23 True Tales of Courage and Character."

Acknowledgments

The author thanks his friends and family for their help and support. Special thanks to W.B. Ignatius and Spence Ingerson for their help in editing and fact-checking the text and to Karen Miles, research assistant. Special thanks to Randall Wright for the design, cover and illustrations, and for the layout of the book, with assistance from Jane Baker and Triad Communications.

Picture Credits

Rick Sowash appreciates the assistance of many sources in illustrating Critters, Flitters and Spitters. In all cases cited below, use was by permission.

Cover design, frontispiece and illustrations by Randall Wright, Wright Designs, Fort Thomas, Kentucky; copyright Rick Sowash Publishing Company.

Trilobite photo: Ohio Department of Natural Resources, Division of Geological Survey.

Woolly Mammoth drawing: (Neg. No. 35935), Courtesy Dept. of Library Services, American Museum of Natural History.

Serpent Mound photo: Ohio Historical Society, photo by Tom Root.

Possum Fable photo: Fred Shaw, Ohio Shawnee Storyteller, in traditional garb.

Little Turtle drawing: Indiana Historical Society, C2582. Note: This is a print of an original oil painting of Little Turtle by the famous American painter Gilbert Stuart. The original hung in the White House but was destroyed when the British seized Washington, D.C. and burned the White House in the War of 1812.

Rienzi photo: Doug Miller, Perry County Historical Society, Somerset, Ohio. Note: This powerful equestrian statue of General Phil Sheridan astride his famous horse named Rienzi adorns the village square of Somerset, Ohio.

Passenger Pigeons photo: Randall Wright, photo of the Cincinnati Zoo's statue of "Martha," the last surviving passenger pigeon.

Wright Family's Robin photo: Rick Wright, photo of the Wright Family home, now on display at Deerfield Village, Dearborn, Michigan.

Cy Gatton photo: Van Wade, great-grandson of Cy Gatton. Note: Cy was about 70 when this photo was taken.

American Bald Eagle photo: Cleveland Museum of Natural History, photograph from the C.M. Shipman Collection. Note: The photo is of Charles Shipman at the Kelley's Island Eagle Nest, 1923. Before the use of an observation tower, this was the only way to observe eagles' nests.

The Wilds photo: The Wilds, Cumberland, Ohio.

Ohio's Elephants photo: Michele Wright.

Ohio Bird Sanctuary photo: Gail Laux, Director of the Ohio Bird Sanctuary.

Toad Tuning photo: Michele Wright.

Canada Geese photo: Randall Wright.

Guide Dogs photo: Randall Wright, with thanks to Pilot Dogs, Columbus, Ohio, for their help and cooperation.

Guide Horses photo: Lisa Carpenter.

Search and Rescue Dog photo: Randall Wright.

Bud the Wonder Dog photo: Phil Niemie, Principal, Bailey Elementary School, Dublin, Ohio.